# What She Really Wants

Marianna

Published by Marianna, 2024.

This is a work of fiction. Similarities to real people, places, or events are entirely coincidental.

WHAT SHE REALLY WANTS

**First edition. October 2, 2024.**



ISBN: 979-8227948502

Written by Marianna.

# Table of Contents

# What She Really Wants
By Marianna Love

# Chapter 1: That Night (Angela)

Let me start by telling you, my real name is Angela Martinez, yes, soy Afro-Latina and very proud. Both of my parents were born on the island of Puerto Rico, my dad being a deep mocha and my mom being a butter pecan tone. Now, I got my amazing facial features from my mom, full juicy lips, big brown eyes, and dimpled cheeks. Not to mention, she blessed me with a thick curvy frame.

I've always had a slim waist, but this backside has always been something, often catching the eyes of grown-ass men, when I was merely a teenager still in high school.

Now, this skin color, I was blessed with my father's deep mocha skin tone, and extremely curly hair and some may even say his temperament, but the fact that my patience for foolishness was almost non-existent, could have been because I am a Taurus, the verdict is still out.

Now, my job as a talent scout sends me all over, especially when my boss, an older White woman named Kathy Schneider does not feel like doing travel during or near the holidays, she'll send me to meet with potential and existing talent.

This time, it was close to the Thanksgiving holidays and there was a singer/actress in New Orleans that she wanted me to go check out. We had seen a viral video of her and wanted to snatch her up before anyone had the chance, thus the reason for me having to be out of town working the weekend before the holidays.

After the meeting with the beautiful talented young lady, I ended up back at the hotel, which was located near the foot of Canal Street.

Exhausted, I stepped out of the cab, handed him my card to pay, and thanked him before I exited the vehicle.

I was wearing a nice pair of high-waisted black slacks with a white long-sleeved fitted shirt and a pair of red heels. I was never one to go with obvious matches, I liked wearing shoes that popped or added a hint of flavor to my outfits.

My cellphone rang, "Shit." I uttered as I entered through the revolving door. It was my kind of boyfriend Corey Myers. I say kind of because we were constantly getting into it over my work.

He didn't like the fact that I would drop everything and just go, when Kathy said, "Go." But that wasn't the case. I had a job, just like he had one and I never gave him shit about how much time and energy he put into his work, as he gave me.

Reluctantly, I answered, "Yes." With a major attitude. "Hey, I was just calling to see how things went." That's what he said, although, I knew he didn't care. We had a big argument before I left for the trip and he had told me, it was my job or him, and since I wasn't wearing his ring and our conversations revolving around marriage often centered around me being this stay-at-home, trophy wife that waited on him and foot, I went my Black behind to New Orleans.

"Things went great." I pressed the button to summon the elevator car. I wasn't in the mood to talk. I wanted to go take off my clothes, get changed, and head out for some of all that good food I smelled while walking downtown, not to mention, a daiquiri or a hurricane had my name on it somewhere.

"I'm about to get on the elevator, so, I'll just call you later after I get settled." I heard him suck his teeth, but he replied, "alright babe."

I entered the elevator and pressed for the 14$^{th}$ floor and proceeded to lean against the wall, the doors re-opened and baby, my whole heart almost stopped. This dark chocolate vision of loveliness with a head full of neatly done locs entered the elevator.

My entire pussy got wet. Now, here me out. One day, I was at a café in Tampa, doing some work on my laptop, trying to be productive, when I saw a table of women laughing. Normally, I mind my business and don't listen to other people's conversations, but when I saw them eye this man with locs as he walked by their table and one of them said, "You haven't fucked, until you've fucked a man with locs."

My ears perked up and I sat and listened in detail. And ever since that moment, I have been intrigued by men with locs. Every time, I see a good-looking one, I always imagine the guy walking up to me, kissing me in the mouth, with his hand on my full breasts, pressing me up against the wall, and fucking the shit out of me.

So naturally, when I looked into his eyes, I sort of blushed at the thought that went through my mind. I gave him the complimentary head nod. He spoke, "How are you doing sis?"

"I'm well," I replied and tried not to have any dirtier thoughts parade across my mind.

To say this man was fine, wouldn't do him justice. Imagine six feet three inches, deep-set sexy ass brown eyes. He had a mustache with a goatee, the beard with about three inches of hang time, these chiseled cheekbones. I looked at his hands and feet and at that point, I was dying on the inside. I started throbbing all over thinking about this man, bending me over and blowing my back clean out.

I cleared my throat, I noticed, he didn't press a button for another floor. When the doors opened, he held out his hand, "After you." Manners, I thought. He walked alongside me for a while and then said, "You following me?"

I laughed, "No, my room is right here." he smiled, "Looks like we're neighbors, at least for a short time."

"It seems we are."

I saw his eyes scan me. Even though I was in those dress pants, my hips and ass did look plump, he gave a side smile. "So, you calling it a night or you up for hanging out a bit, I wanted to go take a walk by the river."

He had read my mind, but I had also wanted much more than a walk. "Um, that sounds great, I can be ready about fifteen."

"Sounds good. I'm Jason." he reached out his hand to shake mine.

"I'm Catalina." Now, when I was younger, I had two dreams, one to grow up and be an actress or become an international spy with the code name Catalina.

"That's pretty ma. I'll see you in fifteen."

I took off those work clothes so fast, I put on some skinny jeans, dark denim, and a fitted long-sleeved gold top. It was a nice temperature out, so I didn't need a jacket, I just added an infinity scarf and put on my tiger print ankle boots.

My hair, I took out of the bun and let the curls fluff out past my shoulders. I was ready. I grabbed my purse, reached inside, and turned my cellphone on silent. I had already made up my mind, I was testing out this guy with locs theory and letting whatever happened in New Orleans, stay in New Orleans.

I heard a knock on my door, I opened it and he was looking good. Nice blue jeans, fitted black shirt, he had this white spacer in his left ear, and I could see the tattoos coming up out of his shirt near his neck. This just got me more excited.

"You ready?" he asked in that smooth baritone. I nodded, walked out, and made sure my door was closed.

***

He walked on the outside edge closet to the curb with this nice bowlegged swag, he'd nudge into me as if we had been dating for months. I smiled.

"What do you wanna do ma?" he asked.

I replied, "I was thinking po-boys, daquiris, and beignets."

I loved the food in New Orleans and I was gonna make sure I ate well.

He nodded, "Sounds good, let's go uptown to New Orleans Seafood and Hamburger and ride the streetcar back." he suggested.

I was feeling his vibe. He was so laid back. He flagged down a cab, he opened the door and I got in before him and we were off.

"So how long you here?" he asked, I saw him checking out the thickness of my thighs. I smiled, "I was going to leave tomorrow, but I can leave Monday if I need an extra day."

He nodded. I looked over at him, "And you?"

"I'm here until Wednesday, I'm a tattoo artist, here for the convention."

That explained the myriad of tattoos I saw under his shirt. I nodded, "That's nice."

"You have any ink?" he asked. I almost laughed. I had always wanted to get one but would chicken out every time, "No. um, not yet."

"You should let me ink you."

"Maybe I'll let you do that," I said that to sound adventurous, but he was going to have to do some serious convincing to get me inked.

He touched a few curls that covered my face and moved my hair back, "You have beautiful skin."

"Thanks. I love your hair." I smiled.

His hand touched my knee, "So, um, what brought you out here?"

"Just some talent scouting."

"Oh, okay, so you're in the industry of music, film?"

"Mostly film, but we do manage some singers. I was here to meet with a singer/actress."

"Nice," he replied. The cab pulled up. He paid and then we got out. As we walked, into the place, he checked me out from behind.

He walked over to the menus and we looked over for a minute. "Oh, I think I might want this seafood platter instead." We headed up to the counter to order and I pulled out my card because I didn't want to assume anything, "Uh-uh ma, put that away."

I laughed and he paid and then we found a table and waited for our food. We talked as we waited; it was something about his smile, the jazz playing in the background, and sipping on wine that just made the night feel perfect.

When the food arrived, we ate and then went to the beignet spot behind the restaurant. We ordered to go and ate as we walked to the streetcar stop.

He stood in front of me, I saw some powdered sugar on the corner of his mouth, I reached up, "Let me get that." I wiped off his mouth with my thumb; he placed his hands on my hips. I placed my hand in his thick luscious mane. He leaned in and kissed my lips, just a soft peck.

We heard the streetcar screech to a stop, the door opened and we got in and found a seat up front. We sat close, hugged up like teenagers courting. I leaned in and kissed his neck, his cologne smelled so good, he laughed and said, "Don't start nothing you can't finish."

"Oh, I always finish what I start," I replied with certainty.

He nodded, "We gone see."

When we got to the foot of Canal Street, we walked along the river, the city was busy, so many college students, but for us, it was just us, he wrapped his arms around me while standing behind me, "Can I take a picture of us? We might not see each other again, but I want to remember you." He pulled out his cellphone and we took some selfies, "We look good." he commented.

"We do."

He placed his hand on my waist, "I bet I could pick you up."

"I'm not as tiny as you think."

"I can squat you."

I mounted his back, "Okay, this is 145 pounds." He squatted me with ease. After laughing for several minutes, he finally put me down. "So, tomorrow, I'm giving you your first tattoo after we have breakfast."

"We're having breakfast?"

"Yeah. Unless—"

"No, it's cool."

"You ready?"

I nodded. I was so ready. Like man, if you don't come on and give me some of that dick.

***

He stood by his door as if he didn't know what I wanted, "Is this good night?" he asked, holding his card key. I took the key from his hand and opened his door and went in. He walked in grinning.

"So."

I walked up to him and immediately began kissing him, pulling off his shirt. His chest filled with ink art, I licked his nipples and kissed his chest. "You wanna take it to the bed?" he asked. And I don't know what happened, I became so wild.

"I want you to fuck me against the wall."

He bit his lip and nodded, he dropped those pants and showed me what he was working with and I got excited. I touched him. He walked me backward until I was pressed against the wall, he undid my pants and peeled them off, then went down.

He opened my legs wider and drank from my cup, using his thumb to tap on my clit and fingers to penetrate, "Shit, papi." I said, the way he used the tip of his tongue to draw and flick my shit, caused my legs to buckle, I wet his face, he stood up wiped his chin. I knew what he wanted. So, I went down, gripped him like I was holding a microphone at a poetry slam and all I had was three minutes and ten seconds to spit my piece.

He held onto my head, he didn't know I was just as gifted with my mouth, he uttered obscenities, "ahhhhhh." He stepped back and lifted me, pressed me on the wall, looked right into my eyes and pushed that long thick masterpiece inside of my pussy, and just paused to let me savor all of him.

My body was already trembling. His eyes locked on mine and knew he was about to tear my shit up. I grinned inside. He started stroking with a nice rhythm and I was tightening my walls on his dick, he smiled just before leaning over and filling his mouth with my left nipple.

He lifted my right leg and dug deeper; my leg started to shake. I felt this wave over my body and I dug my nails into his back and bit his shoulder and said, "Oh fuck."

Then with those strong arms, he lifted me in the air and bounced me on his dick for several minutes, before walking me to the sofa in the suite and laying me down. He looked down at me, placed my right leg over his shoulder, thrusting and grinding, I saw the sweat bead on his forehead, his thumb playing with my gem, and then the ripple went through my body again, this time more intensely. I was shaking and tears formed in my eyes.

He bit his lip and grinned before connecting his chest with my breasts, slowing down his tempo, "You alright ma?" he asked. I nodded. He showered me with kisses along my neck and then started licking my titties.

"My god," I said as I moaned.

He grinned, "You never been fucked like this before?" he asked. I shook my head. I had decent sex with Corey and my first love, but this was some next-level dick. I had never been fucked to tears.

I could feel him picking up his tempo and finally, he pulled out and released on my tummy.

# Chapter 2: The Morning After (Angela)

The morning after, I lay in his bed and you know how you have those weird dreams when you're talking to someone and all of a sudden, they start saying things that don't make sense. Then your face just scrunches like what the fuck? Yeah, I was having such a moment. And for me, it's usually because my subconscious mind is trying to tell me, I need to deal with something on a conscious level...immediately.

My eyes popped open. I wasn't in a panic or anything, however, I was a little disoriented. What I didn't tell you is how I ended up in his bed. So, after he gave me that insane workout, I went to the bathroom to clean up, so I could go to my room. I figured, we hooked up, that was that, you got what you wanted; I got what I wanted, it's a wrap.

No. He met me at the bathroom door, looking all sexy and shit, chest all tatted up, "Where think you going ma?" he asked all smooth leaning against the door frame, dick just swinging.

I replied, "Well—"

He cut me off, "Naw, I meant what I said about tomorrow." He leaned in and presses those full lips against mine and I felt his tongue slip past my teeth. His hands were in my hair, my heart started racing, then he said, "Besides, we're not done yet." He smacked my ass and went into the bathroom. And I went to wait for him in the bed.

Anyway, needless to say, I was a little tired. Suddenly, I had this issue lingering over my head. My actual real life, uh, COREY! Shit. I was supposed to call him last night, but since I was busy...I didn't get a chance to call him,

And Corey is a literal person, if you tell him that you're going to call him back in five minutes; at four minutes and fifty-nine seconds, you better be hitting send on his number. I needed to get to my room.

I sat up, allowed my nicely pedicured feet to touch the soft carpeted floor. I was about to stand, then I saw Jason standing in front of me, "Good morning baby." He leaned over and kissed my mouth.

I smiled, "Good morning."

I stood and he continued to kiss me, I was getting wet all over again, he whispered, "turn around." His hand on my hip, he guided me around and bent me over to where my face and hands were on the bed, then he grabbed my ass, spread me open, plunged into my pool, and proceeded to thrust. I felt his balls hitting against me, his hands on my hips, holding me in place. Slapping my ass, then pausing to lick me before diving back in with his dick. He stood me up, his hand held my hair, not tight, but taunt to one side, while he talked shit in my right ear, "This dick good ain't it baby?"

"Yes."

"You like my shit?"

"Yes."

"It's the best ain't it?"

"Si papi, si."

"Your pussy so good, throw that shit back." He leaned me over again and I proceeded to push back on his dick, while he watched, "Yeah, baby, throw that shit back."

Finally, he released on the top of my ass. I turned to him, he kissed my mouth and said, "Be ready in thirty minutes."

***

I walked into my room frantically, like Angela, girl, the fuck? Okay, I paused. I gathered myself, I looked at my cell, saw all the missed calls and texts from Corey and even, the hotel room phone message flashing.

I dialed his number and he was just extra of course, but I suppose he had a reason, "Geesh Angela, what the hell!"

"I'm sorry. I just literally woke up. I was so tired last night; I ate and fell asleep."

"Work?" he replied. Corey didn't think of my job as actual work. He never understood why I would be exhausted at times. He didn't understand how having conversations with artists that could change the entire course of their lives would be exhausting. Like, bruh...I know, I'm not litigating cases as you do on a daily, but my stuff is just as serious.

"Yes, Corey, work."

"I thought you were flying home today; can I pick you up?"

"Um, I have to meet a client today in a few minutes and I'll be flying in tomorrow, be home around 10:30 in the morning."

He huffed, "So, do you want me to pick you up or?"

"My car is at the airport remember," I replied. His silence reminded him of how much of a baby he acted and didn't drive me to the airport as he would normally do.

He sighed, "Yeah, so I guess, I'll just see you when you get in."

"Okay."

He stayed on the line, "Look Angela, I'm, we'll talk when you get back." The call ended.

I looked at the time, that dialogue ate up ten minutes and I needed at least twenty minutes to deal with the crazy I had going on, on top of my head. I didn't wear my bonnet to sleep, so my curls looked like a hot mess.

I hopped in the shower, did my thing. The hair had to go into a high bun. It was cute with my edges slayed. A light beat on the face, a pair of thick black tights, and a sweater that just barely covered my thick ass.

I heard a knock; I knew that was him. I took a deep breath, grabbed my purse, and headed to the door. He stood there with a big sexy smile,

"You look beautiful." He kissed my cheek. I wondered if he was like that all the time.

"You ready?"

"Yeah."

We ended up eating at the hotel. My meal, a bowl of fresh fruit, a plate with scrambled eggs and wheat toast, and a cup of coffee and some cran-apple juice. He had a spinach omelet with wheat toast and a few glasses of water.

We sat and ate, sort of flirting back and forth. I was out of control like I didn't have a whole man back in Tampa. The sound of jazz played in the background. We talked about places we traveled. He asked me if I was Hispanic and proceeded to speak Spanish to me. I was impressed. He said, "I'm from New York, I lived around mad Dominicans, so, I picked it up."

I was like, "Um, you were trying to holla at those Dominican mamitas."

He immediately blushed, "I mean, you know."

"Yeah, I know."

After breakfast, we walked out to the lobby and stood inside waiting for an Uber to arrive, He had his hands around me like I was his woman. He kissed me and this older couple stopped, "I remember when we were this young and in love. Bless you, both."

We smiled. I said, "We're in love."

He touched my nose, "That's us." He pointed outside. The driver had pulled up.

***

He took me near Armstrong Park, they were having a Second Line. It was lively and festive. If you've never been to a Second Line it's quite an experience. It's a parade in the streets, people walking along with a band out front. Dancing and people were having a great time.

We danced along with the people as if we were from the area. You know when you have flavor, it's not hard to pick up dance moves. We danced until our feet were done.

I was so busy smiling, I didn't realize how far we had ventured off. He smiled, "Dang, we have to go back that way."

"Where are we going?" I asked. He reached for my hand and we started walking back towards Rampart. "My friend has a shop close to here, you ready?"

"Um"

"Come on now, you said last night."

I laughed. I knew what I said, but really didn't think we would still be hanging out after we had our encounter, but there we were on our way to the shop.

We walked in, there were people everywhere waiting to get tatted. A woman, somewhat androgynous, "What's up J." she said smiling.

He hugged her, "Nothing much Sam, this my girl Catalina." I spoke and smiled.

"She's beautiful J."

He grinned, "Is the backroom available?"

"Yeah, no one's back there," she replied as she continued tatting the person in her station.

He walked me back to another area, where there were four rooms. We went in one to the right, "Um sir..." I said with a smile.

He laughed, "I wanna tatt you somewhere private. I didn't figure you wanted people to see."

I looked at him with an eyebrow raised, "Like where?" He pointed to my inner thigh.

"Um I don't know, that might hurt."

"Don't be scared. You probably won't even feel it." He laughed because he knew that was bullshit.

"What are you going to put?" I asked.

"It's a surprise. Trust me."

I pulled down my tights and laid back on this cushioned table, looking up at the distressed ceiling. I was nervous. Thinking, "what the hell am I about to do?" My mother hated tattoos. She was going to flip if she ever got to see it.

He stood by a desk, drawing on that paper. "Just relax, I'm almost done with the design."

"You draw fast."

"I've been doing this for a while. I love my work."

I bit my lip and just looked up. He walked over to me, "Ready?" I wasn't, but I nodded. He placed it on my inner thigh close to my bikini line and peeled back the paper. I saw a little bit of the drawing, beautiful roses, and some cursive lettering.

He looked down into my eyes and started grinning, "You gotta relax ma."

"I'm trying."

He placed his finger on my clit and made circles. Then his finger moved my panties over so the skin from his fingers could make contact. He circled until I got moist and then slipped inside. I smiled and bit my bottom lip. "Close your eyes," he said as he continued to stroke me, fingering me to my delight, "That's it relax, baby." He said and he continued until I quivered and said, "Oooh." He smiled, "You look relaxed now." He leaned over and kissed me.

About two hours later, I had my tattoo cherry popped. He showed it to me with a hand mirror, red roses, with all these beautiful vines and letters, KJA incursive. "What does KJA stand for?" I asked. He gave me a sneaky grin and replied, "Keeping Joy Always."

I smiled, "That's sweet."

He nodded. "You ready?"

***

We ended up going to the seventh ward to a local spot called Cajun's for some crawfish. We sat inside pinching tails and sucking heads like the locals while drinking Big Shot soda, or as they say in NOLA, "cold drinks."

My nose ran something fierce. But the food tasted so good, I just kept eating. After we ate, we went to another spot, ordered daiquiris with shots of patron, and played pool.

Not going to lie, that daquiri was something. I couldn't drink the whole thing. He laughed, "Let me finish it for you lightweight."

I laughed, "Go ahead." My head was so light and airy, felt as if I was floating and not walking.

The sun was beginning to set. I looked into his eyes. The reality of Monday was looming and I wanted to get another taste of him before I left. I whispered, "Let's get back to the hotel." I leaned against him, rubbed his cock, and felt that nice bulge.

He smiled and nodded, "Alright ma."

Even though it was early in the day, I wanted to just spend the last few hours in the room with him. I was going to have to get up early to leave Monday morning.

We were in his room, sitting on the sofa, me in his lap, grinding on him, my breasts in his face. I held his chin and smiled just before sticking my tongue in his mouth. I felt my body tightening and then I whispered, "I'm coming baby."

"I feel you, that's it, ma."

Just as I was climaxing, he lifted me up and then laid me down, as he licked me. My hands in his hair, looking at him work his magic. He wanted me to cum again and I did. He laid on top of me.

The way he looked into my eyes, his hair falling, I moved it back so I could see his magnificent face. His hip motion sent waves throughout my body. This man wasn't just fucking me, he was trying to make me remember that dick for the rest of my life. Like no man that came after him would ever be able to erase the pleasure from my memory bank and I would long to feel like I was feeling in that moment with him until I died.

I started humming. He smiled and then licked my whole tit from the bottom to the nipple. He pulled out and released. I watched him as he jerked, holding himself, trying to act cool. I smiled. He looked over at me, leaned over, and kissed me before getting up.

We were lying together on that sofa, bodies pressed against one another, legs entwined, he touched my arm with his fingertip, "I guess this is it."

"Yeah."

"I hope I showed you a good time."

"It was wonderful." I gave him a peck. "I better go now, so I can pack up." I peeled myself off of him, although, I could have laid there forever or at least another several ho.

He stood up, "Take care of yourself ma."

"You do the same."

# Chapter 3: Back To Reality (Angela)

November 23rd, at approximately 10:30, am, I was back in Tampa. It was time to put Catalina away and bring forth Angela. I took a deep breath and tried to push the memory of that weekend way down in the deepest abyss of my mind, but I had the tattoo and I still had a throb going on from handling all of my mystery loc man's penis. I smiled as I headed to the baggage claim area.

With it being a few days before the holiday, one that I wasn't excited about celebrating, especially since I have indigenous roots, I knew I was going to be expected to perform. And by perform, I mean, being the dutiful girlfriend with Corey to all these functions, which I dreaded.

As soon as I arrived at my car, my cell sounded, I saw Kathy's name pop up, and immediately I thought, *this heifer better not be asking me to go nowhere else for at least another week.* "Hey, special K, what's up?" I said. She loved when I called her that.

"Hey dear, I didn't hear from you, how did it go?"

She was right, I didn't ever call here to say how it went. "Yeah, things got crazy, had to put in a lot of work and extra time, it's done. She's going to sign."

"Awesome, you're the best."

I got inside my car, started the engine, "I guess, I'll—"

"Hold on dear, I hate to ask..."

I was like noooooo, she continued, "I need someone in Orlando for an industry party, nice people, some talent, it's the Saturday after the holiday, so at least, you have time to prepare. What do you say?"

I gave a disturbing smile as I left the parking lot, "Sure." As if I had a choice. It was either her, me, or this one other person we had and they were smart enough to take the rest of the month off.

"Great, talk to you later."

"Urgh," I grunted, but at least, it was a few days after, that way I could have a little downtime.

***

Home, I lived in Ybor City, a nice area in these luxury apartments. Mine was a little over 1200 square feet, but it was more than enough room for me. I walked up to my door and saw roses outside.

It was the sweetest gesture. I retrieved the flowers and read the card, "Sorry about before, love Corey." Not going to lie, it did touch my heart. Corey was a sweetheart when he wasn't being completely ridiculous. He just had some very antiquated ideas about relationships that often led us to butting heads. And since he was a lawyer, our conversations often seemed like were in court defending our viewpoints passionately.

I went inside, placed the flowers on the coffee table, and headed to my room to unpack and repack for Orlando. I called Corey as I headed to my room. He answered cheerfully, "Hey babe."

"Hey, babe. I got the flowers, thank you." I laid my bag on the floor and sat to begin sorting out what needed to be washed and what needed to be put away.

"You like the flowers?"

"I do."

"Are you busy, do you want to go grab a bite?"

"We can do that."

"I'll see you soon."

The call ended and I continued to unpack.

***

I prepared for Corey's arrival. Believe it or not, November in south-central Florida was much different than those of New Orleans. So, I went from jeans and sweaters to wearing a nice airy black, yellow, and white geometrical print dress. The sleeves were long and the cuffs big, but it reached to my mid-thigh and when I tell you I had some serious legs muscles, I kid you not.

I spent a lot of time at the gym, and since I was already on the thicker side, I mainly played up the features I loved. Although, Corey hated it when I wore dresses that showed off my legs. He would always say, "Men are staring."

And I would reply, "so are the women." He would shake his head and just let it go. My hair, I had two afro buns, with a part down the middle.

I went into my bedroom and stopped by my dresser to put on some perfume, Coco Chanel. It smelled lovely on me. I looked at the picture of Corey and me together from when we went to City Walk Park in Orlando. We looked so happy, all smiles. He was truly a handsome guy, low-key, he could have been a model, but his grandfather was a lawyer, his dad was a lawyer, so the only thing he figured he could be was a lawyer.

The doorbell sounded and I went to open the door, and there he stood. Honestly, as mad as he had made me before I left to go to New Orleans, his smile would melt me every time. He was five-eleven, clean-shaven, had these soft brown eyes that would change color in the sun, he was the product of a White mother and a biracial father.

He didn't have a lot of melanin, yet he did have very African-like features. His nose had wider nostrils, his lips were full, and had a pretty peach color. "Hey babe," he said as he threw his arms around me, picking me up slightly.

He wore some beige shorts with a navy-blue t-shirt and some flip-flops. Yes, you can get away with flip-flops in Florida in the fall and sometimes winter, just depends on what part of Florida you live in.

"I missed you," he said as he kissed my neck.

"I've only been gone a few days." I joked.

"I know, but it seems like forever when we fight."

I placed my hands on the sides of his face and brought him closer to me, then suckled his lips. He smiled, "I guess I'm forgiven."

I nodded, "You are. Let's go, I'm starved."

***

Corey drove a black Lexus SUV and it had all the bells and whistles. He made great money, which is why my mother was so star-struck when I told her I was dating a lawyer.

My oldest sister, Lisa had two kids by an African American man in jail and the youngest Julie had just given birth to a child to a mixed-race Latino guy that had three other kids by two other women. So, she was banking on me doing a little better. And, I don't blame her, parents want to be able to tell their friends that their children are doing well. It's like a reflection of their parenting skills. However, I used to tell my mother, "You did right by us. You taught us everything we needed to know. It's our responsibility to do the right things."

Yet, she felt responsible for our choices. It was a weird thing she had going on inside.

We ended up in St. Pete. He didn't want to drive that far, but I convinced him by nibbling on his ear. It was his weakness. I wanted some seafood from the spot that had a NOLA vibe. I know, I still had NOLA on the brain.

We were on the deck eating and talking. "I'm glad you're home for a while. My mom's having dinner. She wants you to come."

I squinted my eyes. I found that hard to believe. She was a nice woman, but through our interactions, I knew she would have preferred Corey settled down with a nice white girl. She thought I was after him for his money.

I should have shown her one of my pay stubs. I made more than Corey. Of course, I never told him that.

I nodded, "Sounds great. But I do have to be in Orlando that Saturday after. I'll be back Sunday afternoon."

"Geesh, Angela, your boss is relentless."

She was but in the best way. She believed in empowering women to be as ambitious and as successful as they could wrap their heads around, and I was for it.

The idea of eating at his mother's house was disturbing my spirit. Our ideas of seasoning were completely different. She referred to my cooking as spicy. And I was like, girl bye, PR food is not spicy. It's flavorful, but spicy, what? And her food to me was just odd and tasteless.

Now, his dad could cook. I don't know why he even let her in the kitchen. Corey did have a sister, that I adored named Katelyn. She told me that I saved her life when it came to hair.

When I first met sis, it was dry and looked ashy, now her curls stay poppin and juicy, "Katelyn and Jerome will be there?" I asked.

"Yeah." He responded. That was cool. I needed some other relatable folks there to help me get through the evening.

After we ate, we went for a walk on the beach. Now, as I stated before, I used to have this curiosity about men with locs and would imagine kinky stuff, but never had I experienced a sensation pulsate throughout my body when one walked by me.

There we were just walking along the shore when this cinnamon-colored man with locs jogged by us and I started throbbing below, I flinched, "Are you okay?" Corey asked. Looking at me with concern.

I stood up straight, "Yes. I'm fine. I, I got a tattoo and I guess I just felt a little shock of pain."

His eyebrow lifted, "A tattoo Angela? You did not."

I nodded, "It's here." I pointed at my inner thigh. He made a face, "You let some guy see you there?"

"Tattoo artists tattoo all kinds of body parts; my inner thigh is no big deal."

I could see the curiosity forming on his face as the questions filled his mind, "What made you decide?"

I shrugged. But I knew. I smiled, "You wanna see it?"

He grinned. I knew he wanted to, but he acted shy a lot of times when it came to stuff like that...he was so proper. I gave him a nudge, "You've seen my area before Corey."

"I know, but there are people out here."

I saw one of the restrooms. I reached for his hand and we walked over to it, "Wait, I can't go in there with you, what will people think?"

I looked around. No one was even looking at us. "What people, come on silly." I pulled him inside and locked the door. Something about having my vagina throb and showing Corey my tattoo in the bathroom made me extremely horny.

I lifted my dress. He looked, "It's pretty, what does KJA mean?" He asked.

"Keep Joy Always," I replied.

He nodded. He was about to open the door, but I wanted to see if his wall game was as good as Jason's.

I stopped him, "Babe, we can't."

I nodded as I reached inside of his shorts and played with him until his dick got hard in my hand, "Can we please. I bit his ear."

"Angela," he said, but the next thing I knew, he was inside of me. I bit his neck, I felt all of him pushing inside of me, we were kissing, his hand on my breasts. I had to be careful with Corey. He liked a delicate balance of wholesome sex with a pinch of kinky. I tried to talk dirty to him once and he was like, "Why are you talking like that?"

"Baby." I moaned.

"What's wrong, should I stop?" he asked. I was like hell Nah, you need to keep stroking, I'm about to cum. And then I came. I held him tightly. He continued and then he buckled in my arms, grunting.

I cleaned up and left the restroom and moments later he met me on the beach. We walked a little longer and talked before heading home.

# Chapter 4: Remembering NOLA (Jay)

Here it was, Saturday, almost a week since I had seen honey in New Orleans. I was hanging out at one of my friend's houses in Orlando. Everyone was in the house, but I decided to take a minute outside on the deck.

I sat there staring at a picture of her, us, in New Orleans on my cellphone remembering that weekend. Believe it or not, I wasn't the type to hook up with just anyone. I had seen her when she walked into the lobby of the hotel.

I pretended I needed something at the front desk, just so I could hear what room she was being checked into. Then I got my room changed to her floor. It was just a coincidence, it ended up being next door. I only wanted to see if our paths would cross, so I could shoot my shot.

As life would have it, it happened. When I stepped on the elevator and saw her face light up, that was a pleasant surprise. It's a weird climate out these days, where men are looked at as predators, and believe me, I get it. Just to see those brown eyes light up, gave me some hope.

"Catalina," I said to myself. Why didn't I ask her for her last name? Maybe, I could have looked her up on the gram. I shook my head disgusted. She said she didn't have any expectations after that weekend. And I don't know, initially, I didn't either, but after vibing with her, I did start to feel something, but how was I going to say that? She might have thought I was weird or a simp, just trying too hard.

My boy Malik walked out, "You alright man, you seem out of it?" Malik and I had been friends since high school, that was my dude and one of the few peeps I trusted with my business. Mainly because he was smart, he would tell you no kind of bull shit just to make you feel good, and also, he wasn't like these new-age dudes, running around spreading gossip and fighting with women on the internet, whack as dudes.

"I'm good man, just out here thinking."

He nodded, "You never told me how New Orleans went." he smiled as if he felt like I was holding something back. I showed him my cellphone, "Catalina is her name."

He looked at the picture for a while. "I met her in New Orleans, she was nice." He handed me back the phone.

"You sure her name is Catalina?"

I nodded, "That's what she gave me, I mean." He pulled out his cellphone and showed me a picture, dark skin, hair was straight though, smile, dimples, those quads, and ass, that was the same woman. "Yeah, that's her."

"She is cool with Cheyenne, they go to those industry parties, meet talent, actors, singers, all that stuff. But her name is Angela Martinez."

I nodded, she gave me another name, that's cool, I didn't tell her my whole name was Kendrick Jason Adams, the initials in her tattoo, I told her stood for keep joy always, but it was my initials, because after that first time, shit, I felt like, it belonged to me.

I belonged to her. I had her name. I just had to figure out a few things. Was she available? Probably not if she gave me another name. It didn't matter because...fuck that dude.

Malik dialed a number, "Hey Chy, when's the last time you heard from Angie? That's what's up, can you get us in, me and my boy Kendrick, you know Jay. Alright, bet." He smiled, "she's going to be at this party tonight checking out talent, bruh."

I smiled real cool like, but inside, shit I was excited, I dapped him, "Thanks, man. Appreciate you."

"I got you, man. You my dawg."

***

Now, I wanted to impress ma, she had only seen me in my casual gear, but a brother had some dressy swag too. I stood in my walk-in closet, surveying my gear. I saw this suit that I had been dying to rock from the Sebastian Cruz Couture line.

It was a red wine-colored button-down shirt, with these champagne-colored dress pants, the vest to match, and my red wine handkerchief. Oh yeah, I was gonna be one of the flyest dudes up in that joint.

I got dressed, put my cologne on, had the nice socks and my shoes, just waiting on Malik to scoop me. I heard the doorbell, I answered the door, immediately my dude, who was also looking fly says, "Damn, don't hurt'em, Kendrick."

I laughed, "You know how we do."

My dude was wearing the white dress pants, gold button-down shirt, the belt buckle matched the design on his loafers. We were ice cold and ready to roll, yes sir. We headed out in his car, the black Kia Optima.

The whole way over, we talked about different stuff, our businesses. He owned a barbershop and a hair supply store and I of course had my tattoo shop. We rolled up to this hotel with valet parking, left the car, and headed in.

Women checked us out, you know, lots of fly ladies were in the place. We checked in with the hostess and they let us in. Malik spotted his girl Chy and we walked over to her, "You remember Jay?"

Chy is Malik's ex, but they remained friends after the breakup, she's a cutie, one of those fair skin girls with that long wavy hair. She smiled, "Of course, I remember Jay, how are you doing?" She gave me one of those church hugs.

"I'm good, and you?"

"I'm good as well" she eyed me suspiciously, "So, Malik was telling me that you know my girl, Angela."

I nodded, "Yeah, I met her in New Orleans last weekend."

"Um. Interesting, well okay, she texted me said she's was close. I didn't mention anything about you being here because she may or may not be bringing Corey. He doesn't usually come to parties, but for some reason, she said, he drove out with her."

I was like, *fuck no*, this is not happening. Malik looked at me, "sorry man." I shrugged it off. I wasn't worried about the dude one way or the other.

Cheyenne smiled, "There's my girl."

I turned and saw her; she was looking right as usual. Black dress with some lace material in front and in back, had her rack sitting up nice and those legs, Lawd have mercy, I got a flashback of giving her that tattoo and smiled.

On her feet, she had these sparkly gold shoes with a design going down the heel, her shoe game was always tight when we hung out. She walked up and our eyes met, she gave me the biggest smile, "Jay?"

"Yeah, It's me." She hugged me. Feeling her that close to me again, sent lil chills down my spine, her hair was straightened, long and flowy down her back, she was all glammed up as they say.

Cheyenne grinned, "So, how do you two know each other? I'ma need this tea."

We grinned.

Angela looked at her and whispered, "I'll tell you about that later."

"Okay. Well, you know Malik," she said.

"Of course, hey Malik." They hugged. Then she stepped back and looked at me.

Cheyenne said with a grin, "And where did you leave Corey?"

"He's visiting with a friend. He wasn't feeling a party."

I was happy to hear that. Cheyenne eyed me, her lips turned over, "I suppose you wanna talk to Angela alone for a minute."

I laughed, "Yeah." We watched her and Malik walk off.

"Wow." She commented as she checked me out. "You look nice."

I nodded and checked her out, "And you are wearing that dress Catalina, or should I call you Angela."

She laughed, "Uh, Angela's fine. Catalina is my alter-ego. My international spy name." she joked.

"Is that right? A spy, nice. So, Angela, I wanna see you tonight."

She blushed, "Jay, I'm here with my boyfriend." That is what she said, but her body language was calling out to me.

"Boyfriend. Um, did you have that when you were in New Orleans?"

"Something like that. I mean, we were fighting and I, I guess, I took advantage of the situation, but I'm back to being Angela."

I nodded, "I hear you ma, is Angela as freaky as Catalina?" I asked.

She whispered, "We have that in common." She stepped close to me, "The weekend I spent with you was the best weekend I ever spent with a man, but I'm already taken and there are plenty of gorgeous women here."

I tilted my head, "I didn't come here for them."

Her eyebrow lifted ad she smiled, "Let me work a little and maybe we can sneak off for a couple of hours, but just a couple."

I watched her strut off to work the room. Malik walked up, placed his hand on my shoulder, "what's up?"

"She said we can sneak off for a few."

He shook my shoulder, "She's into you man."

"What you know about this dude she's with?" I asked.

Malik shrugged, "Dude's like a lawyer for businesses out in the Bay area. You know one of those pretty boys. You can check out her gram, old Boris Kojo, looking ass dude with green eyes."

"Um," I replied. I was far from that type, but you know, a brother ain't never had no issues pulling ladies. I had a few I was still in talks with when I met Angela, but I hadn't called them since that weekend.

I mingled for a while, made some connections, and after about an hour, she found me at the bar, she gave me this sexy ass look, it was all in her eyes. I knew that was my queue. I paid my tab and walked out with her, "Where we going?" she asked.

"We can go to my place," I suggested. I got us an Uber and off we went.

***

The driver pulled up to the gated community where I lived. I had my gate access app open and ready to go, the gate opened and I told the dude to just keep going. I saw ma's face. I said, "Efficient."

"Nothing wrong with that," she replied smiling. When the Uber driver pulled up to my spot, a home I had bought about a year ago, five bedrooms, three and a half baths, the three-car garage where I kept my truck, SUV, and two motorcycles, I thanked the driver before getting out to open her door.

I reached for her hand, nicely done nails, not too long, gold with some bling on the ring finger, "Such a gentleman." she stated, I walked behind her and when we got to the front door, I unlocked it and allowed her to walk in ahead of me, what can I say, I loved to see her coming, and I loved to see her walking away, perfection.

She stepped inside and looked around; I had hired a decorator to do my spot. It wasn't anything too fancy, but I was into Black art, mainly, beautiful pieces of Black women with natural hair. She smiled as she walked around checking out the pictures.

She stopped at my shelf where I had some degrees and certificates, "Kendrick Jason Adams." She turned and stared at me. I couldn't help but laugh.

"Keep Joy Always," I replied.

She turned her lips over, "You know you're wrong for that." she said with a smile.

I stood by the island in the kitchen where I had four white bar stools. She strutted over to me and stood. No words were spoken at the moment like she was just admiring me. I reached for the remote that was at the edge of the counter, played some music, low, H.E.R, Focus played.

"I didn't tell you how handsome you looked." She gave a side smile, which made me blush.

I tilted my head and bit my lip.

"I never expected to see you again," she said.

"I know."

She stepped closer to me, placed her hands on my chest, and just rubbed. "Tell me what you want," I said. She unbuttoned my vest and then my shirt, kissed my neck, and then licked my nipples. I loved the way she would hold my chin, look dead in my eyes and then kiss me, tongue in my mouth, sucking on my lips. She was a great kisser. She stepped back and unzipped her dress. Her beautiful full breasts just spilled out. Immediately, I placed my hands on them, squeezing and pushing them together, while licking from left to right.

I peeled the dress off past those nice hips and it was on the floor, she was still in those gold stilettos. She was about to take them off, but I picked her up by the waist and set her on the island, placing the right foot and then the left one on a bar stool, opened wide so I can examine. She smiled and leaned back.

I tasted ma, she tasted just like I remembered, sweet. The music in the background, my jam came on Every Kind of Way. Her hands in my hair, feeling her body react to my tongue, my fingers, she tried to squirm, but I had her locked in position, I wasn't letting her move until she drenched that spot and she did, legs trying to close on me.

I dropped my pants and found my way inside her, she was so moist from my tongue, and feeling her walls around my penis again, the way she would tighten and hold while I stroked. I scooped her off the counter and held her in my arms.

She belonged in my arms and she knew it, the way she hummed, I carried her to the sofa and sat with the baby in my lap and let her work, she smiled, those dimples were everything. She leaned into me, kissing my ear, my neck, and biting my shoulder, my hands in her. I held the left side of her hair tight and turned her face to me so I could kiss her. I felt her shake, she said, "babyyyyyy." I lifted her and laid on top.

Then I pressed, stroked so slow, digging deep, her leg shook and she grabbed hold of me tightly, I heard her cry out, "shit." I looked down and her eyes were watery, her body still shaking. She shook her head, "Why do you do that?" she asked.

"Because I love it," I replied, then I picked up the cadence, I tried to pull out, but she wrapped her legs around me so tight, I couldn't move. I was like damn babe.

She laughed, "I'm on the pill." I was already sweating, but that move almost made my heart stop.

It wasn't that I didn't want kids, I just wanted to make sure I was married. Yeah, that's right married to the right woman. I felt like Angela could be the right one, but her status was still a little taken, but I was working on that.

Just like in New Orleans, I wound up meeting her in the bathroom and convincing her to stay a little longer. I loved having sex with Angela, but that wasn't the only reason I wanted to see her.

We laid in my king-sized bed talking, "So how long have you been with this lawyer guy?" I asked. Her fingers were making circles on my chest.

"This time, about seven months."

"And the first time?"

"Um, about three months. Our personalities clashed a lot in the beginning and we were still trying to learn each other, hell, we still are." She sat up and looked at me, "And what about you?"

I laughed, "I'm not going to lie. I'm a polyamorous situation." I watched her expression.

She nodded, "So, you see multiple women, how does that work?"

I sat up, "I'm seeing two women, one lives here, the other in Lakeland. They can and do see other people."

She got out of the bed, "Where are you going?" I asked as I got out of the bed and walked over to her. I touched her chin and lifted it, "what's wrong?"

"I don't know. It's almost time for me to leave."

"No, you can't just leave Angela, talk to me," I said.

"I told you in New Orleans that I didn't have any expectations, we could have just left it at that. You showing up and us doing this—" she shook her head, "I don't know."

"I showed up because I wanted to see you and we did this because we wanted to."

She smiled, gave me a cool peck on the lips, and left the room. I followed her out to the living room, where she put on her dress and shoes. She used her cell to request an uber, "I have to go. This was fun and I enjoyed spending time with you. I just don't know what this is or—"

"So, you're not down with Polyamorous relationships, but you cheat on your boyfriend?"

She nodded. I don't even know why I said that. I just didn't want her to leave. "I did cheat on him and that was wrong, but I don't plan on doing it again."

I huffed, "Cancel your Uber, let me drive you to the hotel. I promise to leave you alone."

The drive back to the hotel was quiet. She sat with her right hand in her hair, lips stuck out, "I was out of line. I shouldn't have said that." I apologized trying to get back on her good side.

She gave a side grin and turned to me, "Nah, you said what you said. And just because I didn't like it, doesn't mean, it wasn't true," she replied as she hit my leg playfully.

We pulled up, I parked, she leaned over and kissed me, "I'm still trying to figure stuff out with Corey. I know for a fact he would not be down with a polyamorous situation. He doesn't even like when other men look at me when we're out. Can you just give me some space for a minute to see how things pan out with Corey?"

In my mind, *I was straight up like fuck him, his uncle, his dog, and his goldfish*, but I replied, "Okay ma. We can still be friends though right. I like your vibe."

"Sure, friends."

She got out of the car and I saw Cheyanne hurry over to her before she even got to the door.

# Chapter 5: The Tea (Angela)

Right before Jay dropped me off at the hotel, my girl Cheyenne had sent me a text message saying that Corey had texted her asking if I was still at the party. She covered for me saying I was busy in a meeting with a client.

When I walked to the entrance, Cheyenne met me, she looked as if she was ready to go, "Give me a ride, Angie."

I handed my ticket to the young man working the valet; he went to retrieve my ride. We stood and waited, she nudged me, "You gonna have to spill that tea." She grinned.

"I will."

The car pulled up, my red Nissan Armada, we got in and I drove off, she looked at the side of my head, pushing on my thigh, "Come on sis..."

"You're not going to let this go."

"Hell naw, spill it."

"We met in New Orleans and I don't know, I've always had this fantasy about a guy with locs, so, I wanted to try it on him."

"Fetish?"

"Curiosity, plus, Corey had done worked on my last nerve. I was just acting out. Then, I don't know he was nice and had this cool energy, we were laughing and joking..."

"And sexing," she laughed.

"Yeah, a lot of that. Girl, girl, girl."

"Damn, sis, it was like that?"

"Girl! Even tonight." I sighed, "But, I'm with Corey and he has to respect that. I do too. Plus, he has two other women he's involved with." My face scrunched.

She pushed my leg, "Not trying to share that D, huh sis?"

I shook my head. Especially not D that good, that's the kind of D that make you write a check so bad, the whole economy would collapse. "I have to stay focused on what's already on my plate."

I turned into her neighborhood, "Realistically, I mean, I could keep meeting guys like Jay and vibe, am I going to just keep running from man to man. No. I can't do that. I have to eat what's on my plate and be satisfied."

She made her complimentary face, bottom lip stuck out, with a head nod, "I don't know love, what if your plate is full of beets or cottage cheese?"

I laughed, "Are you referring to Corey as beets and cottage cheese?"

She laughed, "No, but I'm just saying, some people like beets and cottage cheese. But if you like grits and eggs or arroz con pollo...you should get you another plate."

I pulled up to her door, "I hear you." I hugged her and watched her walk to her house and go inside. I blew and drove off.

The whole drive to the hotel, I just kept thinking about Jay. Lawd, he was something and he looked so good in that suit. I bit my lip. The song that we were sexing to came on, Every Kind of Way, by H.E.R., I was getting all flustered and wet. I started singing the lyrics, imagining him in my center, my legs wrapped around his waist, his full lips connected to mine, the scent of his cologne as I would bury my face in his neck moaning and grabbing at his ass, pushing him deeper inside of me.

I turned into the parking garage to park and proceeded to walk to the room. When I got there, I saw Corey in bed asleep. I headed to the bathroom to take a shower.

In the shower, I lathered and scrubbed. I tried to wash him off of me. What was I going to do? No matter how hard I scrubbed, I still felt his touch. His lips on my skin, his hands caressing me, his tongue.

I almost cried. Get it together Angela, I told myself. This is not a game.

Just as I was about to turn off the water, I heard Corey. He entered the shower and he had that naughty look in his eyes like he had a few drinks. That's usually the time, I can get him to do kinky shit, the way I like.

He kissed the back of my shoulder. "I thought you were sleeping," I said. His hands rubbed my thick ass and then massaged my inner thigh.

"I heard you come in and I missed you," he replied as he played with my clit.

I was like, damn, this is about to happen. Not that I didn't welcome sex with Corey. He was always kind and gentle, but my shit was still throbbing from being with Jay.

However, it was clear Corey was in the mood for loving and it wasn't often that I had the pleasure of meeting that kinky version of him, so...

I bit my lip, turned to him, "You wanna be a bad boy?" I asked.

He nodded, "I do."

"Go down," I said. I watched him descend and begin to taste me. When we first started having sex, he acted as if he didn't do oral. He hadn't with any other woman until I went down on him and made his knees buckle. I said, "That's the pleasure of oral."

He licked and played for a while then stood, "Turn around babe." I was like, doggy style, okay Mr. Corey, I see you. I bent over and I felt him gain access. I moaned, "Yeah baby."

He thrust repeatedly holding my hips, then I started throwing it back on him. I could hear him cussing, "shit, oh shit, babe." Don't play with me sir, you came in this shower asking for this.

He reached for me, pulled me up, and grinded, playing with my clit, his left hand traveled up from my navel to my left breast, then he placed his hand on my neck, holding me taunt, I turned my head to kiss him.

My heartbeat so fast. Then I flinched and gushed all over him, "Do you love me, babe?"

"Yes, baby."

"I love you too." Then he came.

# Chapter 6: Mi Familia (Angela)

Now, to understand people, it has always been my notion that you have to understand their upbringing, their family, their religion, the environment in which they existed or currently exist. It has done wonders for me being able to form better relationships with people.

My family, like most, has its issues. However, I could not see myself with any other parents or sisters. It was hump day, December 2nd, I finally left work. I headed to my parents' house for dinner. My mom said she had made sancocho and I was starving and so ready to eat.

My baby sister Julie called me, "Hola hermana, I need a favor," she said. And usually, I knew it had to do with money. My sister got stuck with a bum, for her baby's father.

"Can you stop by the store...." She listed about seven items she needed for the baby. And I was just thinking to myself, *where is that freaking bum, Joel?* But since it was my niece and I loved her; I went to the store to get what she needed.

I went, got all the stuff, and guess who I saw strolling through the store with some young girl, younger than my sister, and my sister was barely twenty years old.

He was dressed in his urban wear, skinny jeans that sag, like, I don't know why that was and still is a thing. I looked at him in total disgust, "Hi Joel, how's your new baby, the one you just had with my sister, the one that I'm buying stuff for because we haven't seen you since she was born."

He rolled his eyes, annoyed that I loud talked him in front of his new prospect, even though, I doubted my words did anything to deter her poor misguided self from sitting on his stick.

"Why you gotta be like this, Angie, come on?"

The girl, also Latina, very thin, her belly all out, with attitude proceeded to get in my face, "Excuse me chica, this is my man and it's not his fault your sister wasn't—"

He looked at her, "Wait for me in the car." She left mumbling some foolishness. He knew I would have torn her narrow ass up. I was a senior in high school when he and my sister were freshmen.

He knew these hands were quick and my mouth was slick.

"Sorry about that Angie."

I sighed, "Joel what are you going to do with yourself? Like seriously." Deep down, he seemed like a nice guy, but he was already on baby number four and only twenty years old.

He shrugged, "I'm trying."

I shook my head, "The only thing you're trying to do is sleep with that girl. And I hope for her sake and your own, that you're buying condoms and use them." I strutted off.

When I pulled up to the house, I saw Julie running out of the garage, her hair pulled up into a messy bun, her hair wasn't kinky like mine. I was the only one that got blessed with the tight curls. Julie and my oldest sister had hair like our mother, sort of wavy. And they also had her skin tone, the butter pecan tone.

She wore a short shirt and a pair of white shorts, "Where's the stuff?" she asked with a sense of urgency.

My face scrunched, "It's in the trunk, calmate." I replied as I unlocked the trunk.

"If mami or papi asks, can I just say that Joel dropped this stuff off?" her brown eyes begged me. It was the second time she had asked me to let him take credit for me supplying his child with basic needs. I nodded and she hugged me.

I went inside through the garage since it was already opened, the smell was amazing, I saw my mother, who looked like she could be our sister. She wore fitted Capri shorts a tank top, and large hoop earrings.

"Hola hija." She said and then hugged me and kissed me, "look what my son-in-law sent me today." This is what she called Corey, even though I wasn't married, but she loved Corey and he could do no wrong in her eyes. When we broke up for two months, she was very instrumental in getting me to give him a second chance.

It was a text gif, "To the prettiest and sweetest mother-in-law."

I smiled, "That's cute ma." She was preparing the bowls. So, I started helping to get it done quicker. I was just hungry and she was taking too long.

My oldest sister walked in with her kids, Michelle age ten, and Marlon age nine. My mom hugged the kids, and spoke to them in Spanish, "Wash your hands and get ready to eat."

They ran off to wash their hands. My sister looked like she was in a funky mood. And when she was like that, I didn't mess with her. She had this thing where she always thought she was right, and I, I was just always right.

"Hey, ma." She hugged our mom, "Where's papi?" she asked.

My mom brought the bowls to the table, "He's in the backyard."

Lisa sat at the table. She was still in her work uniform. She worked at a local clinic checking people in. She looked at me all dressed up and smirked, "Hello Hollywood," she commented.

"Hello, sis," I said as I took my spot at the table.

My father entered, "hola, hola." He looked, "Where's Julie?"

Her voice sounded from down the hall, "I'm coming." A few minutes later, she joined us at the table, "I had to put the baby to sleep."

My dad eyed her, "Did you tell that boy to bring the stuff you needed."

"I did pa, and he brought over earlier."

My dad made a face. He wanted to strangle Joel for getting his youngest daughter pregnant. We all thought Julie was going to pursue her dreams of dancing. She had the opportunity, but she got pregnant and well, she let it go to pursue Joel.

He mumbled something in Spanish, my mother touched his arm and that was his signal to be calm. She began to pray a fiery prayer over the food and finally, we all were able to start eating.

My mom smiled, "You should have brought Corey, hija, I haven't seen him in a while."

My sister sucked her teeth, "You're on the phone with him like all the time ma."

"That's my son-in-law."

She looked at my finger, "She's not married. None of us are. Won't be long before she's walking around here with a little snot-nosed brat like the rest of us."

"She's right, I'm not married. And no child will come from this womb until I am married to a man that is worthy of his legacy being carried on." I eyed her.

"I hate when you do that, start talking all proper, like look at me, I know big words, I've been to college, my boyfriend's a lawyer, blah."

I huffed, "I'm not going to do this with you. You're mad. You're unhappy with the decisions you've made and somehow, that's everyone's fault but your own."

"Fuck you, Angie."

"Hey!!!" My dad's fist hit the table and he said in Spanish, "quiero paz in mi casa." Which is, "I want peace in my house."

It got quiet. I stood up; I couldn't stay. I was annoyed, "I'm going to go kiss the baby before I leave."

My sister commented, "She started it."

***

I went into my sister Julie's room and saw my two-month-old niece Rebecca. She looked so precious. It was truly a shame I thought and I ran my hands over the top of her head of slick black hair. Children are the products of our decisions. They have no say in how they come to be and yet we place so much at their little feet.

Mainly, the responsibility of holding relationships together. That's too much for an innocent child to bear.

I thought about my oldest sister. She had hated me or it seemed. She blamed me for her children's father being incarcerated.

Remember how I said I had serious hips and thighs at a young age that grown men took notice of? Well, her boyfriend was one of them. I can remember when they first started dating, he'd come to our house to hang out with her. Whenever I'd walk into the room, he would always make some comment about my body, "Damn your sister got some big ass titties." Then she'd laugh.

I told her that night, "I don't like when he says that stuff."

"It's a compliment, be chill girl," she replied. Or she'd say, "Wear different clothes." I was like, what the fuck is that supposed to do. My titties are still going to be big and his nasty ass will still find something to say about my body.

She was all in love with him because she thought he was this big-time moneymaker. All he was, was this bottom-shelf drug dealer that had a few coins.

When she finally moved into her apartment, I was glad. Not because she was gone. Honestly, before him, our relationship was so good. I was just happy that I wouldn't have to see him.

But life is so weird. It will reveal the nature of a person's character whether or not, you've chosen to ignore the writings on the wall.

By this time, my sister was pregnant with Michelle and already had Marlon. She asked me to watch the baby while she ran some errands. Now, my sister and this guy had been getting into it a lot. So, I was under the impression that they were done.

I was babysitting. The front door opened, I walked into the living room to see him and my whole heart sank. You know how you just get uneasy around certain people; he gave me that feeling.

"My sister isn't here. She'll be back in a little while." I said. I picked up my backpack. I was going to let him stay there with his child.

He walked over to where I stood, brooding over me, "You ain't got to leave."

"I know, I have homework and stuff, so—"

"Why do you act like you are scared of me?"

At that moment, I honestly wanted to cry. He was a tall guy and even though he was relatively skinny, I knew if he hit me or got on top of me that it just wasn't going to be a good situation.

I laughed, "I'm not scared. We cool." But he still stood in front of me looking at me, licking his lips.

"I like you, Angie, you're pretty. I've always thought you were the prettiest of the sisters."

Now, I was back to feeling uncomfortable. I was quiet. Praying that Lisa would walk in and this crazy man would get away from me.

"I'm only 16 years old."

He laughed, "You old enough to know better." He reached and grabbed my breasts and I slapped his hand. "Oh, you trying to act like you don't like the attention."

"I don't." I headed for the door and he ran to get in front of me, "Can you please just let me leave." My eyes watered, "please."

He laughed at me, grabbed both of my arms, and tossed me onto the sofa, clawing and grabbing at my clothes.

He pulled up my shirt and started licking my breasts and then he tried to undo my pants. The door opened. She literally saw him on top of me and heard me crying and only said, "What are you two doing?"

Like hello, he's trying to fucking rape me. He got up, "She's trying to you know, but I told her, you'd get mad."

"You fucking liar." I fixed my clothes. "I fucking hate you. I hope you fucking die. Mierda pinche cabron." I grabbed my stuff and left her apartment. As I was walking down the street, she ran behind me, grabbed my arm.

"Are you going to tell dad?"

I shook my head, my eyes still filled with tears, "I'm okay if that's what you wanted to ask."

She made a face, "I just don't want there to be any trouble. You know this guy and the people he runs with. If dad does something to him and then, what if the hurt dad."

She knew how to manipulate me. I adored our father. And if I would have told him what her lousy man did to me, my dad would have handled him. I didn't want anything to happen to my father.

I replied, "I'm never babysitting at your place again. You bring the baby to our house." She nodded and I walked off.

A year later, this fool raped a fourteen-year-old in the same apartment complex. The people were trying to put him away. They ask around for anyone else who was assaulted by him. Just so happens that day, when he tried his shit with me, I had started recording with my cellphone in my bookbag.

It was the nail in the coffin for him and things between Lisa and I had not been the same.

Julie entered the bedroom. I turned to see her staring at me. "I'm glad to have you as my big sister." She hugged me tightly. "One of these days, I'm going to make you proud."

"I'm proud to have you as my sister. I only want you to focus on things that are right for you and the baby. We don't get to choose how we come into this world, but once we're here, we should make a point to do the things that fulfill us."

She nodded, "it's probably not going to work out with Joel." The realization must have hit her.

"He's just not ready. And you're not obligated to sit around waiting on him. Do *you*. And that doesn't mean go out and throw yourself into another relationship. It means, find you. Whatever makes you happy."

After talking with my baby sister, I said goodbye to my parents. As I headed to my car, my sister Lisa stopped me, stood in front of me. And I was like, okay, what is this all about, do you want to cuss me out some more, tell me how it's my fault your man is in jail, tell me it's my fault why you can't foster positive relationships?

Suddenly, her eyes just welled with tears and she threw her arms around me. There was a heaviness she had been carrying and I felt it. It caused me to cry with her. "I'm so sorry Angie. I knew and I didn't say anything. If I hadn't come home," she sobbed, "how do I look my children in the eyes and tell them, what he did to you, that girl? It's horrible."

"When they are ready to have that conversation, we'll do it together, but right now, just let them enjoy the innocence of being children."

"I've been talking to a counselor. I know that sometimes I'm shitty to you, but that's my bullshit. What you said tonight was true. I'm unhappy and I have been. And I've carried his sins for way too long."

"Then stop," I said. "You don't owe him anything," I added. She hugged me and then I left.

# Chapter 7: The Follow Up (Jay)

Now, I had followed ma on Instagram, just to get a feel for where she and this dude relationship was headed. I didn't want to crowd her space. I just wanted to see, what kind of pictures she posted. She didn't post a whole lot with him on her page.

I guess it was more of her industry-related stuff, her with celebrities, her at parties, you know. On his page, he posted pictures of them together. My impression of the dude was, he was an alright-looking guy, but he wasn't me. And I knew what Angela wanted, even though she wouldn't come right out and say it.

We were in New Orleans walking downtown, I asked her why she never pursued acting if her degree was in Fine Arts. She said, "I didn't have the look. Agents kept saying, how do we market you?"

She played it safe.

My cellphone sounded, Chy called, I answered, "What's up Chy?"

"She said that she's coming, but, He's coming along with some friends of his. Sorry." Her voice sounded with sympathy, but I wasn't worried.

"You good. I'll see you tonight."

I put my phone on the counter. I had a guy coming in to finish off a sleeve and then I was going to take off the rest of the day to go check out Cheyenne's new spot. She opened a café with a stage to promote local talent in the area. All I needed was a diversion so I could spend some time with Angela.

The shop door opened. I saw one of my, situations walk in, her name Yvonne, she was the Caribbean, had this deep dark skin. It was one of the things she felt most insecure about herself, but the thing, I found most attractive.

She had a plate of food in hand as she approached me, "I brought you some food," she kissed my cheek. This was usually her way of telling me, I haven't seen you in a while, what's up?

Even though we were in a polyamorous situation, she had a little jealous side. When she felt I was spending too much time with other people, she would make her presence known, like, I'm still here.

I took the food, jerk chicken, rice, and peas with salad. She could cook her ass off. She was on the heavier side of girls I'd normally date, but as I said, her skin color was so magnificent, I couldn't let her pass by.

"Thank you, smells so good."

She smiled, she had a slight gap between her two front teeth, she wore her hair cut short and curly. "I was hoping we could hang out tonight."

I blew out a bunch of air, "I have something going on tonight, I can't."

She placed her hand on her hip, "Maybe I should just stop trying." I tilted my head. I knew she was not about to act up in my place of business. "I handed her the food, take this to my office, I'll be back in a second."

I looked at one of my partners, "I'll be back man." He grinned as he continued to tattoo his customer.

I walked into my office and saw her sitting at my desk, "What's this all about?"

She pouted, "I don't know. I have just been feeling lonely."

"What about your other friend?" I asked. I liked that he kept her busy, so I could pursue other things.

But then she said, "I broke it off with him."

I nodded. That was different. I sighed. I walked around to her, she rose to her feet, "Can you just." She said as she rubbed my crotch. I knew she just wanted me to beat it up right quick.

She was wearing one of those long flowy dresses. I just picked her up, laid her out on my desk, pulled those panties to the side. I reached in my drawer and wrapped it up right quick. Because, I didn't want to think she would try to trap me, but I wasn't about to chance it.

Thick and juicy, I held those hips in place and dug deep inside. She called my name while I pushed deeper, then grabbed those breasts, squeezed, I played with her clit and then she creamed all over me. I pulled out, took off the condom, and sat in my chair, "Finish me off baby, I want that mouth."

She grabbed my shit and devoured it, it disappeared in her mouth, deep throated my dick, "I grabbed onto the armrests, my toes tried to curl in my shoes, "Shit." I said and finally, she caught it in her mouth.

I was still breathing heavily when she said, "I'm in love with you Kendrick. That's why I broke up with my friend. I only want you."

I knew how she felt. She wanted me, but I wanted someone else. It's crazy how the world deals us cards we didn't ask for. I cleaned myself up with some wipes I had at my desk. "I hear you and I get it, but I'm not at that point yet. If it's a problem—"

"It's okay. Maybe in a few months." She smiled, kissed my cheek, and left.

I watched her leave, fuck. That was insane. I liked Yvonne and I cared about her, but she wasn't the one. I figured that out after New Orleans.

I was out with Angela one night and there were these street performers, he walked up to us, "I'll give you this 100-dollar bill if you can out sing me." Now, I wasn't a singer, but I could do a lil something. When the dude opened his mouth, I was like ain't no way I'm topping that. But then Angela opened her mouth, singing Lauryn Hill's version of *Can't Take My Eyes off of You*.

When I tell you, people were gathering around, clapping and singing along, it was dope. I had fun that night. I said, "You should be a star." She gave me a little push.

All I knew was, I couldn't wait to see her. I gathered myself and started humming the words to the song as I walked back out to my workstation.

****

The night had arrived, I sat in the back with some of my dudes. Cheyenne was doing her thing and getting people to sign up for open mic. I saw it when Angela walked in wearing an all-black fitted jumpsuit that hugged her curves. Malik nudged my elbow. I knew exactly what he meant. I said to myself, "Damn why did she do me like that?"

She was with him and two other people, a guy, and a lady. I stood up and boldly walked over, "Hi, I'm a friend of Cheyenne's," I said as I looked into Angela's eyes.

She had this smile in her eyes like, "Why are you playing?" but she went along, "Hi a friend of Cheyenne, I too am a friend of Cheyenne and this is my boyfriend Corey and his friend Ryan and Ryan's girlfriend, Stacy."

I shook their hands. I could see the dude looking at me all suspicious-like. "There's a table close by, over here." I pointed to the one that was next to the one I sat."

I saw him look around for another spot, but there wasn't any if they wanted to sit together. They walked over and sat. Cheyenne pinched my arm, "Behave."

"I am. You just need to figure out how to get me fifteen minutes alone with Angela."

She shook her head and walked off.

The talent portion began. I could see the dude on his phone and talking with his friend. She tapped his shoulder and whispered in his ear. He placed his phone down on the table.

Cheyenne went on stage after a guitarist finished and said, "This next person, you're going to love. She holds a place near and dear to my heart, my girl Angela Martinez."

Angela looked around and shook her head, "no." But Cheyenne got the crowd to call her name until she stood up and slowly walked to the stage, she looked at Cheyenne and whispered something in her ear.

Watching her on stage, she moved her hair out of her face and stood in front of the mic. She cleared her throat, closed her eyes, took a deep breath, and sang Jill Scott's, *He loves Me*.

She pulled the crowd in, her voice, people were bobbing their heads, recording my girl and her dude looked shocked, as if he had no idea she could sing. Like how are you in a relationship with a woman that can sing and never had her serenade you? I shook my head.

When she finished the crowd clapped like crazy. I walked up to the table, "Great job."

"Thank you."

I looked at him, "You're a lucky man to have a beautiful woman sign to you like that."

He nodded and looked at her. That's when this white guy walked up, "Wow Angie, I had no idea."

She stood up to hug him, "Matt, what are you doing here?"

"Checking out talent, that's what we do right. I had no idea that you'd be one of the talented people here."

"She's one of them," I said.

He handed her his card, "If Kathy isn't going to sign you, you should call me."

She smiled, "Aren't you in Miami now?"

He nodded, "I am, but there are some great opportunities down there. Don't sleep. I'll let you all get back to your evening." He left.

"That's cool, you should call him."

He cleared his throat, "Angie already has a job and she's not moving to Miami. We live in Tampa."

I smirked and walked off because he didn't want these hands.

My name was called. So, I went to the stage. I smiled, "I haven't done this in a while. Um, I wrote a poem after meeting this amazingly intelligent beautiful woman. I hope y'all like it," The First Time

I still remember the first time our brown eyes met

I spoke and said, "hello."

She smiled and the melodious alto flowed past those full raspberry-stained lips to reply, "Hi."

It was something about the look in her eyes

Her stance, the way she filled those sexy black pants

The red shoes, ma, was a whole mood

She intrigued me

I wanted to know the thoughts that dwelled deep within her mind

What made her laugh, cry?

I wanted this woman with all that divine feminine essence to bless me with her presence

I remember the first time our lips touched

And our tongues danced a beautiful dance

I remember her soft hands caressing my chest and my back

I remember the way she played in my hair as I tasted her sweet nectar

The way she bit lip and said, "ooooh shit."

I remember the first time I made her leg tremble

And how she nearly collapsed from the words I wrote with the tip of my tongue

How I held her up, pressed against the wall just before I took the plunge

I remember her receiving me; like she needed me

Her walls tightly squeezed

Savoring every stroke

My face buried in her pillows

Then licking each one

I remember the way she sounded when she reached her peak

I will always remember because she is impossible to forget.

I got a lot of people clapping and whistling. I could see the look in her eye as I walked by her table. I had recited that poem for her, just like she had sung that song for me.

I had Cheyenne get her to go somewhere and talk like she was having a crisis. I pretended to leave with my boys, making sure I stopped at his table to shake his hand, "Have a nice night."

"Thanks." He replied.

***

I walked into the storeroom, where all the extra supplies were kept. There was another room with a door that closed. I walked in and saw her with Chy. When she saw me, her eyes smiled and she gave me this sexy look.

Cheyenne said, "I'll leave you two to um, talk..." The door shut and I locked it.

She eyed me, "So, what's this all about?"

"You already know."

"I loved your poem."

"I wrote it for you."

By this time, she was up on me, touching my face, her lips touched mine, "I thought we were going to behave for a while."

"I never agreed to that."

She chuckled and kissed my neck, "We don't have a lot of time."

I unzipped the jumper in front and slid that thing down, her breasts looked nice sitting up in a red laced bra and her ass, right in the matching thong. "Against the wall," I said.

She grinned as she walked backward and leaned against the wall. I touched her. I knew she would be wet and she was. I played with that thing until she grabbed my hand. I licked my finger and then kissed her so she could taste how sweet she was.

I lifted her leg and just like that first time when she asked me to do it to her against the wall, I did. But this time, I didn't have the leisure of time. I had a lot to cover, so I was moving on all cylinders, licking, squeezing, and stroking, the only crazy thing was, I had already busted earlier. And usually, the second one took a little longer to release.

I thrust and pushed inside, stroking as our lives depended on it, she moaned in my ear, grabbed my ass, and bit my shoulder. I was sweating. She tried to control her sounds.

There was a tap, "Hurry up." Cheyenne whispered.

I slowed down and looked into her eyes, "I love you, Angela." I could see her eyes water.

She held me tight and replied, "I love you too." I felt it, it was right there, I sped up, and finally, it happened, I erupted. We kissed, panting and still enjoying the feeling, "I have to go," she said.

I nodded as I watched her scramble to leave the room.

# Chapter 8: Realization (Angela)

The drive from Orlando back to Tampa opened my eyes. Corey and I sat in front, his friends in the backseat. Naturally, I was still on a high from singing in front of an audience, so I sang a few tunes while we cruised.

Stacy said, "Oh my goodness Angela your voice is amazing."

I smiled, "Thank you. That's nice of you."

Corey stared ahead. He had this look on his face.

The guy added, "Angie the rock star." I relished the idea of it. I giggled.

"You should call that guy Matt, see what happens."

Corey huffed, "Angie isn't going to Miami. We live in Tampa. Besides, her voice isn't like that, and she doesn't have the look those people are looking for.

My eyes squinted and I stared ahead. I wasn't the kind of person to snap on my man in public. But I did have some words floating around in my head.

He touched my leg, "Our lives are in Tampa." he smiled. I nodded. I was annoyed on the inside. My mind flashed back to that dreaded holiday dinner at his parents' house.

Before we went, I was getting ready in the bathroom, I had done this beautiful twist out. My hair looked so full and shiny. He came into the bathroom, "Are you going to do something to your hair?"

I wanted to slap him. Sir, what did you think I was doing in here for the last thirty minutes? He knew I was annoyed. He tried to correct himself, "I was hoping you could do it like the day we first met."

He wanted my hair straightened. That meant another 45 minutes on my hair because my curls were rebellious, which was why I rarely straightened my hair.

Then we got to his parent's home and his mother added insult to injury, "You did your hair."

I was like bitch my hair stays done and I'm always fly. Corey's sister just shook her head. Being that she had a kinky texture of hair, she was often victim to their mother's microaggressions.

We arrived at Corey's place and said our farewells to his friends. He walked towards his house and I walked towards my car. "Angie where are you going?"

"I'm tired. You have an early flight tomorrow, so—"

"Okay, what did I do now?"

"I'm still waiting for you to see me in this relationship."

"What does that even mean?"

"I'm not that good, I don't have a look?"

"Just because you let some street thug that probably only wants to fuck you put ideas in your head, I'm the bad guy."

"He wasn't the only one that said I was good. And even if I don't plan on going to Miami, it would be nice to have my man believe in me." My eyes were filled with tears.

"Angie will you just stop. Please."

I nodded; he just didn't realize how tired I was of constantly dealing with my feelings being invalidated.

"You're right," I replied, I unlocked my car and opened the door.

His face was a picture of confusion, "What are you doing?"

I turned the key in the ignition, "Going home."

"If you leave this time Angie, I swear."

I shut my door and backed out. He watched in sheer disbelief as I drove away.

# Chapter 9: Leap of Faith (Angela)

Three days after Corey and I disagreed, I blocked him. On everything. It was the first time I had taken such a drastic measure, but I didn't want to fall back into the same cycle.

I had also done the forbidden of not responding to my mother. I avoided her like I was a cat and she was a tub of water. This, of course, led to some very angry messages being left on my phone.

I called my father and asked to see him somewhere privately. He met me at a library in Tampa.

The look on his handsome yet stern face spoke volumes. My father knew me well. And as soon as he saw me sitting at the table, his eyes covered me with love.

I stood to greet him. My hair poofed out, my face buried in his chest. He could tell I was carrying something heavy.

"Que te pasa m'ija?" Which is what's wrong?

I stepped back, "Moms going to hate me."

He gave a soft smile and responded, "Your mother will never hate you. Be mad, but hate, no."

"I can't give her what she wants and I have to see what's out there for me."

He nodded, rubbing his beard, "When you were a little girl and I'd watch you act out scenes from movies, singing, and dancing, I always felt you would be a star."

"Really?"

"Yes. I've just been waiting on you to go after what you want." he placed his hands on my shoulders. "You only get one life to live, it would be a shame if you spent it doing things other people wanted."

I smiled. My father was the true picture of divine masculinity. He was a protector and a provider and he always encouraged us to be ourselves.

After our conversation, I walked away feeling better and still feeling scared at the decision I had made.

I talked to Matt about the Miami thing and he said there was work for me if I was willing to put in the effort to audition.

I told Kathy that I was resigning. Her jaw almost dropped, "You can't. Just...go and see what's out there, and if it doesn't work out, come back in a month."

I agreed.

The next thing I did was, change my number and went off the grid. I didn't want any distractions while auditioning for work.

Matt had given me a place to stay in Miami. Said it was an investment property that was just sitting. I agreed to move in by the end of the week and hit the ground running.

That weekend, I auditioned for the role of a witch in a web series. The role of a teacher and the role of a spy. Out of the three, I was hoping for the spy role. She was a badass character and some scenes would be filmed in Mexico.

In addition, I had booked some print ad stuff for hair and booked a few fashion shows.

Was I a big-time star? No. But I was doing something that I enjoyed. And the break from everything and everyone was so welcomed.

***

About a week later, I was contacted about the role of playing the witch. It was scheduled to start filming the week before Christmas.

I figured I should go hang out a little before my schedule got hectic. On the real, I was seriously out on the prowl and wanted something without any attachments. My main goal was my career and not getting into a full-blown relationship.

It was Miami, I knew there were salsa clubs everywhere. I got dressed in these camo tights that laced up on the sides, high-waisted with a white half tank, and ventured to a nice salsa club. Curls were on fleek, face slayed. As soon as I walked in I broke a few necks. I saw this mixed-race Latino, about six feet tall, with this nicely trimmed beard checking me out.

This White guy walked up to me, asked me to dance merengue. We dance and the whole time I could feel papi's eyes on me, like oh, you wanna Twix.

For some reason, I typically caught the eye of light skin Puerto Rican men. My first love Andres was that high yellow complexion. He was my first, freshman year in college.

As soon as a salsa song sounded, and the guy I danced with thanked me, there was papi, holding his hand out, "Would you like to dance?" he asked as if he was sure the answer would be "yes." I smiled and gave him a shot.

He was a good dancer. He knew how to lead and make a girl feel pretty. When a bachata sounded, someone walked up, he shook his head, no. He kept me for the entire five songs. "How did you learn to dance like this?" he asked.

"Soy boricua."

His eyebrows raised, then he started speaking to me in Spanish. At the end of the night, I looked into his soft brown eyes, "Do you have a girlfriend at home?"

"No."

"So, do you want to hang out some more or—"

"We can go to my place."

So we headed to his apartment, I looked around to get a vibe. Nothing unusual, clean, no weird odors. He poured me a glass of wine, we talk for a while and then I'm like, it's getting late and I really want some, so I can go home and get some sleep.

So, I straddled him while still wearing my pants, but I was wearing tights and a thong, so I could feel all of him bulging in those jeans.

He smiled, "Damn mami." I stuck my tongue in his mouth, while I dry-humped the shit out of him. I wanted to climax first just in case his stroke game was weak.

I rocked back and forth, we kissed. He was a good kisser like he knew how to use his tongue. I felt it coming and I moaned. He lifted me and laid me on his sofa, then peeled off my pants, surveying me.

"It's pretty," he said as he looked at my paradise. I didn't know what to say to that. I just smiled. He leaned over, lifted my shirt, and started licking my breasts from the bottom to the nipple. I could tell he was a breast man by how he played with my tits with his tongue and squeezed them.

He drizzled kisses down my chest to my belly just before he started playing with my clit, tapping it with his thumb and fingering with two fingers. Then he tasted. His tongue game was no joke. I had to grab his face. He laughed, "Damn mami, you taste sweet." He stood up and took off his pants. I watched him play with himself.

I bit my lip, "Do you have condoms?" I asked. I was on the pill, but this was a random fuck.

He looked confused, but I was prepared. I sat up, looked in my purse, and pulled one out. He stood in front, I took his dick and licked the tip, then the shaft. I wasn't trying to hook him, so gave him my level one oral game.

Then I put the condom on him. He sat on the sofa, "Come here." He wanted me to ride him. I allowed him to fill me and immediately he started licking and kissing my breasts. Then his hands were on my ass, squeezing and moving me to his liking. "Oh shit, mami, ay dios mio." He held me tightly for a moment like he was trying not to cum, "hold up." He slapped my ass and moved around to the back. His hands spread my ass and he licked up and down making my leg shake.

Then I felt him penetrating, his hands on my hips, holding me steady. Then opening my cheeks wider, pushing in deeper, his hands went around and played with my clit until I let out a moan tightened my walls on him, he moaned, aarrrhhhhhh" and it was done. He pulled out and went to dispose of the condom, when he returned, I was dressed.

"Are you leaving?" He asked. I nodded, "I have a crazy day tomorrow."

He walked over and kissed my mouth, "When can I see you again?"

Now, I was only looking for a hookup. And I was certain, he was only saying that because he didn't want to seem like a dog. I replied, "You don't have to play the game."

"What game?"

I chuckled, the one where you pretend like you want to see me again, and then you never call. It's cool. I just got outta something."

He kissed my mouth, his hand on the small of my back. "I'm not looking for anything serious either, but I enjoyed this time with you and I would love to experience it a few more times."

We both smiled, "I'm a cool dude, I can cook, I dance, and you already know what my mouth do."

I nodded. "I have the next few days, but after that my schedule gets crazy."

His hands were in my hair, he kissed my mouth again, allowing his hands to travel to my breasts. "You should spend the night, it's late."

I smiled and ended up sleeping at his place.

It was Saturday morning; I was lying in Javier's bed on my side. He liked to spoon, so he was pressed against me, his arm wrapped around me. I moved a little and he got even closer, his lips showering kisses on my neck, "Buenos dias, mamita." he whispered as he felt my left breast.

I giggled, "Good morning." He was horny and morning sex sessions were some of my favorites.

I felt him kissing and licking down my spine, he bit my right cheek and then kissed it, just before spreading me open and tasting me from behind, his attention to detail was impeccable, the way he traced with the tip of his tongue and wiggled his finger on my gem, I pulled at the sheets, "Javi." I called out his name. He continued until I flooded his face.

I felt his hands squeeze my ass, he kissed both cheeks before spreading them wide, I felt him enter me. While I was flat on my belly, he kissed my neck while grinding from behind. I cussed because I didn't want him to fuck me like that. I wasn't trying to get hooked on his shit.

He kept pushing and grinding, like every time I whined, "shit." He went deeper. He bit my neck and started sucking. I was like, um um, I'm the one that usually bites. He pulled out and asked me to turn over, he laid on top of me and continued with those slow stokes and grinding, my legs wrapped around him, my hands caressed his back, while I matched his rhythm grinding underneath, he leaned in and kissed me in the mouth and then started sucking my nipples when he started thrusting faster, I knew he was about to erupt, he pulled out and I grabbed his dick and sucked it until I felt his juices on my tongue.

I was in the shower, I had to rinse off since I would be getting an Uber back to the condo I was staying at. I didn't want to be smelling like something crazy in someone's car.

When I got out of the shower and went back to his room, he had laid out a pair of gray sweat pants and a long-sleeved University of Miami t-shirt. I got dressed, grabbed my stuff, and found him in the kitchen making revoltillo, basically an omelet... he had eggs, onions, green peppers, chopped ham, and potatoes. It did smell good, I smiled, "So you really can cook."

He set a plate on the counter of the island, "Eat before you go." he said. I sat on one of the bar stools and he sat next to me, "So, Angela, what do you do?"

"Um, well, before I moved here a few weeks ago, I was a talent scout, finding talent for my agency, actors, singers, models, people to represent."

He nodded, "And now?"

I had to laugh because I had never said out loud, "I'm an actress."

He smiled, "Nice. I honestly thought you looked familiar."

He pulled out his cellphone and pulled up a print ad I had done with an athletic company, "This is you?"

I smiled, "Yeah, wow, it's up already."

His soft brown eyes covered me, "That's why I kept looking at you last night. I saw this ad when I was looking for something for my sister and I was like, damn, honey is nice."

"Um, so you saved my picture." I gave him a nudge.

He laughed, "I hope you don't think it's weird. I was just like; I'm going to post her as my woman crush Wednesday."

I laughed, "That's sweet. So, what about you?" I watched him speak, he had pretty lips.

"I went to that school." He pointed at the shirt I wore. "for finance, now I work at an investment firm, so if you ever need any investment advice."

"That's what's up. I will have you look over a few things." I looked at his refrigerator and noticed a picture of a little boy. "Is that your nephew?" I asked.

He smiled, "That's my son, Marco."

"He's handsome."

"Thank you. Any kids?" he asked me. I shook my head. "Do you want kids?" he asked.

I nodded, "Yeah, one day. I'm not in a rush. I want to have one with the right person."

He nodded. I was curious, so I asked, "Are you and his mother still friends, what's the status?"

He hesitated, "We were both young. And things just didn't work out." he replied, but somehow, I felt like there was more to the story...

# Chapter 10: What Happened? (Jay)

Sunday, December 20th, I was chillin at the crib with my dude M. I held a nice fat one to my lips, sucked in, held for a second, and blew out, I passed it to him, "I still haven't heard from her," I said.

He had asked me if I had heard from Angie. It was like she just disappeared. Cheyenne hadn't even heard from her. Her social media pages didn't have any recent posts and her number was not working. And I wasn't the kind of guy to crowd a woman's space, I just wanted to make sure she was okay.

I mean, the last time I saw her, we had snuck off and did some kinky shit while her man was in the same building. I didn't know if he found out and went stupid. The thought to make that drive to Tampa danced around in my head more times than a dozen. Plus, I was just missing her.

He passed it back to me and said, "So, what you gone do?"

Shit, what could I do? She knew that I was feeling her. I had told her I loved her. And that wasn't something that I had said to any of the women I was involved with at the time. "I have no idea man." Honestly, I was feeling some kind of way that she just ghosted me.

My cellphone sounded. I received a call from the gate guards asking if it was okay for a woman named Trish Anderson to visit. Now that was something. Trish was the woman I dated who lived in Lakeland. She had a son and we had been on a pause for a minute because she was supposedly trying to work things out with the father of her child.

"Yeah, it's fine," I said to the man over the phone.

M looked at me, "You got company?" he grinned.

I nodded and shook my head, "It's Trish."

He made a face. I chuckled, "Yeah, I know."

He stood up, "I guess, I'll get out of your hair." he said laughing, "I'll stop by on Christmas, you need me to bring anything?"

"Just whatever you sipping on." We dapped, hugged and I walked him to the door. As he was getting into his ride, I saw Trish's red Honda coming toward my house. She pulled into the driveway and got out of her car wearing these loose-fitting beige pants and a tank with a white sweater. She was a slim, cocoa brown honey. We had met several months ago at a grown and sexy party.

I noticed her sitting alone staring at her phone. She was one of those cute quiet-looking types. I had it in my head that girls like her were low-key freaky. We talked for a minute and she was nice. She told me she had a kid and worked as a nurse and that she didn't usually hang out.

After a few dates, we started kicking it pretty heavily. This didn't make Yvonne happy because even though we were both doing our own thing, she had a jealous streak, especially since Trish was younger and slimmer.

She walked up to me and kissed me on the cheek, "Hey, what's going on?" I asked.

"I just wanted to see you." She replied. I walked her to the door and we went inside.

We sat on the couch, watching Netflix, well, she was watching, I was feeling a buzz. She wasn't the kind of woman that initiated sex, so I was just sitting there feeling like, maybe? I moved closer to her, kissed her neck. She smiled and turned to me. I placed my lips on her, no tongue. She told me she wasn't into that. I kept placing kisses on her neck, felt her modest breasts, and squeezed before letting my hand slip into her pants and started playing with her clit.

She started to moan, I said, "You want it?" she nodded. I stood, dropped my pants. She was already laying down ready for me to get on top. I was like naw, you gone work for this dick tonight. I sat down, "Get on top." Slowly she mounted me, she almost acted embarrassed to have to get on top. She wasn't anything like Yvonne who was down for anything or like Angela who was hella freaky and aggressive in bed. She would grab my face while riding me, look right in my eyes and ask me, "You like this pussy?"

She rode me and she was nice and tight, so it felt fucking good and it had been a while since I was deep in anyone. It felt like I was about to bust. I slowed her hip movement with my hands and I felt her, she started hollering my name, "Kendrick!" I lifted her in the air and bounced her on my dick until I felt close, I pulled out and it was done.

She asked to stay the night, I didn't mind. It was already late. That night, she told me that her kid's father met someone else and proposed marriage. She was feeling down and didn't want to be alone for the next few days.

The next morning, I woke up, she was already up. I heard her in the kitchen. I went took my shower because I had clients coming into the shop, I was going to have a busy day.

After getting ready, I went into the kitchen, I saw she had made breakfast, some eggs, toast, turkey bacon. She was sitting at the island eating while looking at a catalog on her phone. I saw a picture of a woman, thick and fine as hell, her curves reminded me of Angela. I looked over her shoulder, "What's that?" I asked, trying to get a closer look.

She turned her lip, "Just this company down in Miami, they sell nice clothes. I wish I had a body like hers." she said. Trish had a bad habit of comparing herself to other women, which often made her seem insecure.

"Your body is fine the way it is," I said. I kissed her forehead. But as I'm looking at the picture, the hair, the dimples, the skin, that was my Angela. So, now, I got more questions, "What store is that?"

"Tre -shiek."

I made a mental note. So that's what it was, she finally stepped out and went after what she wanted. "I made you some food," she said as he pointed to a plate already fixed up.

I grabbed it and started eating, "So what are your plans?" I asked. I wasn't trying to kick her out, but I needed to know how long she was going to be in Orlando. For two reasons, my parents were arriving in a few days and I didn't want my mother getting any ideas about me settling down just yet. And also, I wanted to make a trip to Miami.

"Oh, I was going to stay," she walked over to me and hugged me "for a few days, I can stay longer if you want."

My forehead got hot, "Um, I'm going to have people coming and going in a few days, my schedule will be busy, you know."

"It's okay. I'm flexible. I'll just stay out of your hair. I just really don't want to be by myself for the holiday."

I was like, "Noooo." How could I say to her, "Get out?" I didn't want to be mean. Then she did something that blew my mind. She touched my crotch and started playing with my penis, then the next thing I knew, she was on her knees with her mouth on my dick, licking and sucking. Granted, her skills needed some work, but damn, I was like, she must not want to be alone because Trish didn't like oral at all. She thought it was nasty.

After that, I left her at my place and went to work.

# Chapter 11: Baby Mama Drama: (Angela)

After spending a few days with Javi, my schedule got crazy. I was on set nightly filming for my role as a witch and by day, I was working with a personal trainer preparing for the role as a spy.

It was late, I was in my trailer going over my lines for my last scene. I was starving and ready to be done. I was hoping that the director would not be special. My cellphone sounded, I answered, it was Javi, "Hola mamita, can I see you tonight?" he asked.

I smiled, "Uh, I don't know what time I'll be finished here. It's already late. I still need a shower and I'm starving."

"Just come. I cooked."

"Are you sure?"

"Yeah, I'll be up. I'm wrapping gifts for my son and nieces."

"Okay."

It was almost 11:30 when I finally washed all the makeup off my face, changed, and left the location. I arrived at Javi's place at midnight.

He opened the door wearing basketball shorts and a ribbed t-shirt, showing off his arms. He immediately kissed me in the mouth, which provoked my smile. He was freaky. Like, his kisses were always with tongue, his hands in my hair, feeling on my ass.

"It smells good in here," I said, I placed my stuff down by the coffee table. He had his tree up with gifts underneath. "Look at you, not bad," I commented checking out a gift he had wrapped.

He smiled, "It took me forever to wrap that one gift." He walked into the kitchen, "Are you still hungry?" he asked.

I was like…what changed from the time I spoke to you to now, hell yeah, I'm hungry. "Yes." I replied as I walked into his kitchen, "Oohhh arroz con gandules and pernil. You know how to spoil a girl."

He fixed me a plate of food, "Here you go mamita." I took it and sat at the counter. He joined me but didn't eat.

He looked at me, "How was your day?"

"Crazy." I laughed, "But tomorrow should be better. I just feel so tired in my body."

"Have you decided on what you're doing for the holidays?"

I took a deep breath and responded, "I want to go to Tampa to see my family, but I kind of left on shaky terms and—"

"Scared to get back to deal with the aftermath."

"Yeah. It's a lot of stuff, but sooner or later…"

After I finished, he took my plate, cleared it, and placed it in the dishwasher, "We should go to the hot tub, no one should be in there."

"Isn't the area closed?" I asked. He nodded, but I got the hookup and can go in whenever I want. He rubbed my shoulders and it felt so good. I didn't have to be anywhere super early, so I was like, "Okay, let's go."

The area was a gym, with a pool and a small hot tub. He locked the entrance once we were inside. I was wearing my underwear since I didn't have a swimsuit available. He had on his trunks.

He sat and then I got in and straddled him, his face lit up, "I like this."

I bit my lip, "I thought you might."

His hands reached for my breasts, he moved my strap out of the way and exposed the left, and began to lick my nipple with the tip of his tongue. Then he did the other, then pushed them together burying his face in my breasts. I laughed, "I love breasts." he said proudly.

"I can tell. Is that what caught your eye that night?" I asked.

He nodded, "Yeah, and just the way you walked in, just owning the whole room. I was like damn, mami is fucking hot. What'd you think about me?" he asked.

"Well, I was thinking, he's fine, but he's probably like most of the guys that look like him, with the shits." We laughed.

"Dang, the shits. I was at one point."

"Is that why you're not with the mother of your child?"

"Uh, sort of, but like, I was not cheating on her. She was just too jealous and always thinking I was up to something and believe me, I gave her no reason to think like that. She had it good."

"And she gave up all this," I touched him and stroked with my left hand. He placed his hand on my chin and pulled me in for a kiss, the other hand touched my clit, he wiggled it until I climaxed, I moaned in his ear, "shit papi."

He pulled out his penis and I mounted him. Our sounds echoed in the space. His hands held me tightly while I grinded on him, "I want to taste you," he said as he lifted me, set me on the edge of the tub, and traveled down and began to lick and as soon as I climaxed again, he penetrated me, my hands touched his chest, he had this serious face he would make like I'm about to tear it up. He lifted me and bounced me up and down. I looked into his eyes and grinned, "you like how I fuck you?" he asked.

I nodded, "I do." He released one leg and held the other up while still stroking, we kissed while he administered those slow strokes.

"I'm about to cum," he said. He pulled out and I stroked him with my hand and licked his shaft until it flowed from him.

The next day, I was sleeping and I heard a commotion. My eyes opened, I looked around, he wasn't in the bed. I heard a woman's voice, and suddenly she got loud, "This is fucked up Javier. How can you have another woman in your bed?"

I was like, ah fuck no, not the baby mama drama. I got up, looked for my clothes, and put them on just in case I would have to throw hands. I didn't want to do it butt naked.

"No. Damn it, Lauren. Stop." I heard him scold.

I heard a little boy cry, "Mommy, please stop."

"Shut up Marco." She fussed.

"Don't talk to my son like that."

"He's my son too."

"Then act like it and stop acting like a child."

"Tell that bitch to come out here. I swear Javier. I still love you, please," she begged.

I heard his voice lower and finally, heard the door open then shut. Slowly, I walked out to the living room. I saw him with his hand on the door. "Hey," I said.

He turned to me slowly, "Hey. Sorry about all that."

I nodded. As much as I was starting to feel him, I wasn't digging that drama. I had enough already. He walked up to me, "I was about to make some breakfast."

In my head I thought, *how are you going to act like everything is cool? I'm not crazy. That chick wasn't acting like that for no reason.* "When was the last time you had sex with her?" I asked.

His face. He hesitated. I nodded, "And that's why she's here trying to tear up your shit because you're giving her hope. Every time you lay with her for whatever reason, she's thinking...there's still a chance."

"So what do you want me to do?" he asked.

I shook my head, "It's not about what I want. It's about you making a choice and standing by it." I looked at the time, "I have to go."

I headed towards the door, "Angie wait." He walked over to me, "I like you."

I sighed. I liked him too, but I still had so many unresolved feelings floating around in my head.

"Right now, maybe we just take a pause and, in a few months, if you've figured out this whole situation, we can try again." I kissed his mouth and left.

When I got home, I took a shower, as I stood there with the music blaring singing the song I sang that night in Cheyenne's café, I realized, it was time to go to Tampa and just be blunt. Corey deserved an explanation.

My mother deserved to hear from me that my life was my own to live. As I pondered fifty million ways the conversations and interactions would go, I thought about my time with Jay. I wondered if he even still thought of me.

I got out of the shower and made up my mind to make the trip home.

# Chapter 12: What A Day (Jay)

It was Christmas Eve; my parents flew down from New York, my mother Diane Adams and pops Khalil Adams. The whole way from the airport, I was trying to figure out a way to explain my relationship status with Trish before we got to my house.

Trish was posted up in my spot like the woman of the house. Honestly, it didn't look like she had any intentions of leaving. The only thing I knew for certain, that after Christmas vacation, she had to get back to her child and her job.

My mom and dad didn't believe in all the new stuff we young folks were experimenting with, but to be honest, it wasn't anything new...we just called it something different. Anyway, they weren't going to be cool with me just shacking up with a woman, unless I had intentions of marrying her.

I looked my mother in the eyes, just before we went through the gate, "Mom, uh, I have a friend that's visiting for a few days."

Immediately, her face scrunched, "Is this friend a woman?" she asked sternly.

I nodded. She looked back at my father, "Ya hear this Khalil, your son is out here shacking up with a woman."

My dad looked at me through the rearview, "Is this girl you're staying with, your girlfriend or—"

"We're in a relationship, but she stays at her place. She wanted to visit for the holidays, her people live in North Carolina."

My mother rolled her eyes, "I don't know what's going on with you young people today. You meet a girl, you like the girl, why not just get married and stop playing house." She fussed until I pulled into the garage.

My father got out, opened the car door for my mom, and helped her out. I grabbed the bags. As soon as we went inside, Trish was standing in the kitchen, "Hi." Her face glowed.

My mother, smiled, "Hello dear."

"I'm Kendrick's girlfriend," she said. I was like wait, what, but I wasn't about to get into that in front of my parents.

My mom hugged her and smiled, "You're so pretty." She turned to my father, "This is Jay's father, Khalil."

He hugged her, "Nice to meet you."

Trish smiled, "I can show them to the room."

My mother smiled and responded, "It's okay, we always stay in the same room when we visit." My dad grabbed the bags and they went off to the room.

Me I looked at Trish, confused. "You told my mom you were my girlfriend."

She nodded, "Well, I kind of am. I always tell people that we're in a relationship."

I shook my head, "Trish."

"Look Kendrick, don't start. We've been having a great time. Don't ruin it."

I threw my hands up, "I have to get to the shop for a quick appointment. I'll be back in a couple of hours. My parents usually take a nap for a couple of hours, so you don't have to worry about them."

She nodded. That was my way of trying to tell her not to fill my mother's head with any more ideas. I left the house and headed to the shop.

Christmas eve, the shop was a little crazy, I couldn't believe so many people were out getting tattoos. I had one client that I needed to touch up and I was heading back to the house.

So, I was sitting, working on this touch-up, when suddenly, I hear someone ask for me, "Where is Kendrick Adams?" The dude called my government name. I knew it was about to be some bullshit. I looked into the lobby. I see my receptionist arguing with pretty boy Corey.

I excused myself from the client and walked to the lobby, "What's good?" I asked staring at him. He stood about arm's distance away, face all bawled up like he wanted to square up.

He pointed at me, "Where's Angie?"

I laughed, "You're asking me where your woman is?" I shrugged, "how I'm supposed to know that?"

"Don't fuck with me. I saw how you kept looking at her that night. You want Angie, but she's mine."

"Look man, this is my business, you can't come in here with all that. Now if Angie wanted you to know where she was, she would have told you."

He swung on me, I stepped back, grabbed his arm, turned him around, and placed him in a chokehold, he squirmed and tried to break free. "Calm down, calm down." He stopped moving. "Alright, you good?" I asked. He couldn't talk. He nodded as best as he could and tapped my arm. I released him slowly.

"You're just a thug. Angie could never be interested in a guy like you."

I smirked if he only knew. He walked outside and I followed him, just before he got in his car, "Angie and I met in New Orleans and that poem I recited that night...that was about her." I winked and walked back into the shop.

I almost felt bad about crushing his spirit, but he had that shit coming. I went and finished my client's tattoo and then went home.

The whole drive home, I wished I had a way to contact Angie. I was dying to see her. And I wasn't in the mood for any bull shit. I walked inside, I saw my mother and Trish all chummy.

The house smelled nice though. My mom had started cooking and I was hungry. "You want something to eat," my mom asked, as she stirred a pot of beef stew.

I nodded, "yes ma," she noticed when my moods were off, "you alright?" she asked.

"Yes ma'am." I sat at the counter. She placed a bowl in front of me, "here you go."

Then she looked at Trish, "there was a visitor that came by earlier."

Trish made a face like she didn't know what my mother was talking about. "Who came by?" I asked Trish, I knew only a few people had access to just stop by unannounced.

She shrugged, "It was a delivery lady, she had the wrong address."

I nodded and went back to eating my stew.

# Chapter 13: The Chaos (Angie)

I've always been the kind of person to own up to my bullshit, no matter how fucked up it was. So, as I was taking that drive from Orlando to Tampa, licking my wounds, I wasn't mad at Jay, but I did feel some type of way. Just because I owned my bull, didn't mean, I was happy about it.

I had not contacted him when I went to Miami and I knew he had his stuff going on. It just took me by surprise when I showed up at his place and he already had a woman living with him.

I thought about that last night we spent together before everything went to shit. He told me he loved me. I took him seriously. I believed him. Shit, I felt it in my gut. But, I guess, time doesn't wait for any man or woman. So, there I was, on my way home to deal with the aftermath of my decision to break up with Corey and move to Miami. I did have a trunk full of gifts, nice ones, hoping that a few trinkets and baubles would help soften my mother up.

The music played as I drove, I was close to the exit for my mother's but, I choose to keep going until I got home. I needed a minute to pump myself up.

I got to my apartment. Actually, I kind of missed my place. Walked around my living room, stopped in front of the sofa plopped down, and just sat. I talked to myself, "You're grown, Angie. It's your life. Now get up and go face your mother." Slowly, I stood to my feet. I wanted to move, but my feet were stuck. I laughed, "Okay, I got this." Then my feet moved and before I knew it, I was out the door headed to my parents' place.

When I pulled up, I saw my little sister Julie outside with her baby's father Joel. I got out of the car, she ran up to me, "Angela." She wrapped her arms around me tightly, "Where have you been?"

"In Miami working?" I replied.

"Ay dios mio, you look smaller, have you lost weight?" She asked.

I laughed, "Just a little. I've been working with a trainer for a new role." I smiled.

"My sister, the actress." She said. Julie and I would always put on little shows for the family.

I was reluctant to go inside, "How are things?" I asked.

She chuckled, "Well, you know, mami is still a little angry, but I can tell she misses you. She looks at her phone all the time like she's waiting on you to call."

That was a good sign. Maybe she would not snap my head off. I nodded, "I guess, I better go in and say hello." I walked past Joel and eyed him.

He smiled, "I'm trying to do better Angie."

"Umm hmmm," I replied as I went inside.

My niece and nephew ran to me, "Tia!!!"

I hugged them, "I have gifts in the car." I handed my niece the key, "Go get the gifts out of the car and lock it."

Eagerly, they ran off to get the gifts. My dad walked up to me, kissed my forehead. "Welcome home hija." I smiled. I looked over at my mom, who pretended not to see or hear me as she was in the kitchen. He nudged me.

I walked over to her and stood next to her, "Hi ma," I said.

"Could you please tell your daughter that I'm not speaking to her?"

"No." My father replied.

She looked at me, "So, your little dream didn't work out, now you're back wanting everyone to forgive you." She said with her hand on her hip.

"I'm not looking for forgiveness. Just acceptance." I replied.

She scoffed, "I just don't get why you would leave a perfectly good man that can take care of you, to do what, run around doing god knows what."

"Acting is a job. It's a very lucrative one at that. Besides, I was already taking care of myself. I've been doing that since I left this house. I don't need Corey to take care of me. I only needed him to see me and respect me."

"He's a good man."

"Yeah. He's a good man, just not the right one for me. I'm sorry you feel let down by all of this. I just can't make an important decision about my life just so you can have something to brag to your friends about."

Her eyes watered. She cussed in Spanish and left the kitchen. My sister Lisa walked up, "Welcome to the disappointing daughter crew." I couldn't help but laugh.

"Don't worry, in a few months, she'll be fine." My sister said. "Now, what did you get me for Christmas?" she asked.

The kids were putting the gifts under the tree. I pointed, "Go see for yourself."

She hurried over to the tree, found the gift with her name on it, and opened, a small box, she opened it to find a set of keys. "What's this?" she asked.

"Look on the back of the key," I said. There was an address.

She jumped up and down, "No fucking way Angela, you bought that house down the street."

I nodded. I knew how much she wanted a house close to our parents' house so the kids could have a place to go easily after school on days she worked late. The house was in foreclosure, so I got it at a great price.

She started crying, "I don't deserve this."

I walked over to her and hugged her, "Stop. You are a hard-working mother that sacrifices a lot for your children. Whatever happened in the past between us, is done. I want my sister back."

"Tia, you got us a house?" asked my niece.

I nodded. "I can't wait to see my room."

She added. "Me too." Said, my nephew.

My dad smiled, "That was very nice of you m'ija."

I left my parents' house around 1:00 am. I got to my apartment around 1:30. As soon as I got home, I saw Corey waiting by my door. I took a deep breath and approached with my key in hand, "Hey." I said as I stepped around him to unlock my door.

He followed me inside. "I would say Merry Christmas, but this has been the worst Christmas of my life," he said.

I was like, geesh, here we go. I decided to let him get everything off his chest. I was going to play the role of the bad person in his story and he was determined to let me know.

"I was good to you and this is how you repay me. I don't get you, Angie. You want to throw everything we have away for some thug?"

I was confused, "What are you talking about?" I asked.

"I know about you and that guy and how you two met in New Orleans. He told me all about it. I was here trying to work on us and you were there fucking some other guy like a whore."

My face got so heated, "Look what you not going do is call me any type of bitch or whore or anything that's not my name."

"So, you don't deny you slept with him, he's the one that put that tattoo down there, seriously fuck Angie." His face got redder by the second, "Is that what you want some thug?"

"Jay is not a thug and I'm not seeing Jay. I've been living in Miami. Doing the thing you said I didn't have any talent to do."

It was silent. He shook his head, "So, now, you want to be an actress...a singer...you're going to move to LA next, this is insane. We were good."

"No, *you* were good. You want me to make myself small so you can feel big. You didn't even know my degree is in Fine Arts, which means, I've always wanted to be a performer, but that's not important to you...you just want me barefoot and pregnant, waiting on you like a servant."

"I never treated you like that."

"Yes. You have. Every time you tell me my dreams don't matter and that I have to settle for what you want because you're the man. When you tell me things like you don't like my curly hair or when I act ethnically. Like what the fuck Corey, it's like you want to strip me of everything I am, just so you can be happy...then what about me?"

"My mom was right; you don't deserve me. There are so many women that would appreciate a man like me."

Then you should go be with one of them" I replied. And I don't know why, but I felt pain in my mouth. It happened in a flash.

I looked up in his face, "Angie, oh my God, I'm sorry."

My lip dripped with blood. He tried to get close to me. I pulled out a knife, "Don't. get the fuck out!"

He continued to approach me, "I swear to God, I will stab you, get out!" I walked toward him. He backed up until he was at the door and he left. I locked my door and went to the bathroom to look at my lip.

Swollen, a small cut on the inside. It would probably be healed before I had to be back on set. I thought about calling my dad, but I just let it go. I was still pissed. Cheyenne called me, I answered, "How did it go?" she asked.

I walked into my room and sat on my bed, "Girl, my mom is still mad, but you know what, after how Corey just hit me, I'm glad I ended it."

She shrieked, "He did what!"

"Calm down. I'm okay." I was still in my clothes. I stood to take off my pants, and then my shirt, then laid in my bed.

"I can't believe he hit you." She said still shocked.

He had. I couldn't believe it myself. I would have never imagined his hands touching me in that way. I knew he loved me, but I didn't know if that was a precursor to what was to come in our relationship. Lord knows I had always been outspoken. If that simple statement made him do that, Lord only telling what he was capable of if we got into a heated discussion revolving around something else.

# Chapter 14 Going Back: Angela

I went back to Miami, but this time, I found my own place. I had been working and doing well, which afforded me the chance to secure a beachfront place, not far from where Matt had let me stay. He hooked me up with the realtor and I got a fairly decent deal on the property.

I learned. A lot of opportunities were not by chance, but by the acquaintances you had and the ones they had.

It was now springtime. I had just finished shooting in Mexico, playing the role of a badass spy. I had lost fifteen pounds, which was a lot to me, I was used to my fuller frame and thickness, but this new look had me looking hella badass. I mean, my abs had abs. I was seriously ripped.

There I was walking and I decided to walk into this Cuban spot for a bite to eat and I saw this man in a business suit looking hella delicious and I had a familiar feeling. Our eyes connected and we both smiled.

Now, he stood next to a woman that appeared to be into him and when she noticed him checking me out, she scowled at me. I looked away with a grin. I saw them order and head to a table. Then I ordered and took my food to go.

I left the restaurant and I heard my name, "Angela." I stopped and turn to see Javier. My face lit up because he looked good and honestly, I hadn't had any since he and I parted ways before Christmas.

"Javi," I said.

He smiled, "Hey, how have you been?"

"Good. I just got back a few days ago and you?"

"Good. Good. I've been wanting to call you—"

"And what happened?"

He chuckled, "I didn't know if you still wanted to see me after that last time. I messed up big time."

"Did you figure out your situation?" I asked. Hoping he'd say "yes."

He nodded, "Yeah. I got custody of my son. And she and I don't mess around anymore. Just realized that my son didn't need to be raised in a toxic environment."

"That's awesome. I'm happy for you both."

"So, can I see you maybe tonight or this weekend?"

I looked inside the restaurant. The woman he was with pretended not to be bothered, but I saw her watching us when I turned to look. "What about?" I asked.

"She's a coworker and she's married. We're just having lunch."

I nodded, "Okay. So just call me and we'll link up." I replied.

His eyes danced across my skin. I laughed. He smiled, "You look great. I mean, you've always looked great, I can't wait to see you."

I watched him walk back to the restaurant.

***

The night began with Javier coming to my place to pick me up. Then we went to this Latin club to dance. The place was popping, had a nice crowd, everyone danced, had drinks.

Javier and I were on the floor, naturally, because we both loved to dance. Now, of course, since the nature of our history, I allowed him to get closer to me and touch me more sensually. I supposed this guy watched how I danced with Javier, figured he was allowed those same liberties.

Javier went to the bar. And I was on my way to the table, this guy walked up to me and asked me to dance. The song was a bachata and he kept trying to get nasty. I said to him in Spanish, "please stop."

He got angry, "You let that other guy dance with you, touching all on your ass."

I was like, "that's my fucking business, you can't."

He tried to hit me, but, ya girl had been taking self-defense classes for my role as a spy, I grabbed his wrist, twisted it, and damn near broke it.

"Fucking puta." He said and walked off.

Javier grabbed him, "Is there a fucking problem?"

The man shook his head. Javier pushed him, "You alright?" he asked me.

"Yeah. I'm good can we just leave," I said. I was no longer in the mood for dancing.

We went near my place and walked on the beach for a while. The water was still a little cool as it ran across our feet. We talked. I told him about my Christmas and everything that transpired between Corey and me.

"He hit you. Damn. That's messed up," he said.

"Yeah. It was, but it's over. my mom finally is okay about us not being together, especially after he told her what happened. I wasn't going to, but I guess he was trying to get her to see his side." I sighed and stopped, looking into his eyes, "I won't pretend as if I was innocent in everything. I believe in owning my mistakes."

He nodded, "That's what I like about you. You're so straight up. It's like, I don't have to guess about what you want. You say what you mean and mean what you say."

I bit my lip and reached for his belt loops, pulled him close, he looked down into my eyes and I pressed my lips against his, then whispered, "I want you." He smiled.

We ended up back at my place, as soon as we stepped inside, I placed my hand on the back of his neck and gave him a serious look, leaned in and French kissed him while undoing his pants with my right hand. I pulled out his penis and stroked him until I felt him grow in my hand.

"Let's go to your room," he said. I turned and started the walk to my bedroom, which was right off the living room. He followed me.

He stood by the foot of my bed, watching me get undressed, I laughed, "Are you going to keep your clothes on?" I asked.

He shook his head, "I just wanted to look at you. I miss looking at you." He said and then he removed his clothes and got in the bed, "Come sit on my face," he said.

I was like, okay sir, you did not come to play games. I straddled his face; his hands cupped my ass and he drank from my cup. I almost forgot how gifted he was, my whole body felt a tingle and I felt like I was going to collapse. I held myself up against the headboard until he stopped.

He moved from under me and I felt his hand on my ass, "Come here." He wanted my ass in the air. He had one of those ribbed penises, and every time he stroked, I could feel this sensation on my walls. He controlled my hips, moving slowly like he was enjoying the view. I heard him moaning and savoring me as I enjoyed him. I started pushing back on him and he cussed, "Fuck mami."

With Javi and I, it always felt like we were trying to show each other, who could out fuck the other, he pulled my leg and I felt the weight of him as he was lying on my back grinding, a finger circling my clit and one hand on my right breast, as he pushed deeper.

He pulled out and I turned around. He looked down at me, licked his fingers then rubbed me before penetrating again. He leaned over and began showering me with kisses all over my neck and wildly licking and sucking my nipples. I held him close, I watched him move his hips, the motion was hypnotizing, "Oh my God Javi, papi." I moaned. He smiled and bit his lip and went faster until he melted right there in my arms.

I could feel his heartbeat against my chest. We both glistened, panted, moaned, and cussed from the sensation we both felt. He rolled off of me and just laid there for a moment. I turned and looked at him and laughed because he looked so out of it, "Are you okay?" I joked just before getting out of bed.

"I'm good, just need to catch my breath."

The next morning, I got up, but he was still tired, so I let him sleep in. I was in the kitchen on facetime with Cheyenne when he walked in without his shirt, "Um who is that?" she asked. I turned and saw Javier.

"Javier," I replied. Javier waived. I picked up the phone, "I'll call you back later."

"You better."

He walked over to me placed his hands on my hips and kissed me, "I have to go get my son from my mom's."

"Okay," I replied.

He looked into my eyes, "If you're not doing anything later, maybe you can stop by and watch some movies with us."

I smiled. He wanted me to meet his son. But were we on that level yet? "Are you sure?" I asked.

He smiled, "Yeah. I mean, Marco is cool, I can just say you're my friend."

"Umm hmmm," I replied. "Okay. Friend." I chuckled.

He kissed me again, "He usually goes to bed around 8:00 pm, so..."

"And what are we going to do when he goes to sleep because you're loud." I joked.

His eyebrows lifted, "Me loud, no you. Especially when I put that tongue on you," he replied.

That part was true. "We'll just have to be quiet," he said kissing my neck. "I'll see you tonight."

I watched him leave and, at that moment, I felt relaxed and had a good vibe about the possibility of us. But time would only tell.

# Chapter 15: Calling It Quits (Angela)

I had spent several nights with Javier and his son, under the guise that I was just a friend and even though we had not put labels on what we were doing, it almost felt like we were in an actual relationship. The tricky part was waking up in the morning, so I could leave before his son found me lying in his bed.

Javier didn't see a problem with this, but for me, if we were just dating casually, I didn't want his son thinking I was filling the role of bonus mom if I wasn't going to be around.

After a few weeks of this, I was at his house, sitting on the sofa with Marco, teaching him to play chess, while Javier worked on a project for his job. Marco had the prettiest gray eyes, his skin was a creamy white complexion, and his hair straight, tapered on the sides and longer in the front.

He looked at the board, "I got your king." He said excitedly. He had won.

I smiled, "Looks like you beat me." I reached out my hand and we shook.

"Great game," he said. He yawned, "I think I'm sleepy now, can you read me a story?" he asked as he sat there in his little Miami dolphin pjs.

I smiled, "Of course."

"Let's go to my room." He walked over to his father that was sitting at the table staring at a laptop and talking on the phone. "Good night papi," he said and kissed Javier.

"Your mom wants to say goodnight," he said to Marco.

But Marco had not heard from her in a while, so, he was a little in his feelings and said, "No. I don't want to talk.

Angie's going to read my story now."

I heard her squeal, "Who the fuck is Angie? Who do you have around my son?"

He stood up and went into the bedroom and I took Marco to his room and read the story.

After I read to him, I tucked him in, "Goodnight, Marco." I said, I turned on his night light, he reached for me, this melted my heart, I hugged him.

His little voice sounded in my ears, "Goodnight, Angie."

When I left his room, I heard Javier still in his room arguing with his ex. I went into the living room and sat down on the couch. I sat for a while, drifting off when he walked in, "hey." he said. I looked into his eyes and saw the aggravation.

"Is everything cool?" I asked. I knew it wasn't. I had been flying under the radar. She didn't know about me. As far as she knew, Javier was not seeing anyone seriously. And truly, it wasn't serious, but if I was around her son, perhaps she thought it was more serious than it was.

He nodded, but he looked defeated. I stood up, "Maybe, I should just leave."

He walked over to me, "No. I want you to stay." He kissed my lips. "Let's go take a shower, he grinned.

After a few times of trying to make love quietly and waking up his son, we figured, we could carry on in the shower without causing too much ruckus.

We're in the shower, kissing passionately, his hands are all over me and mine all over him, the water was nice and warm as it cascaded down our skin. He brought my leg up and penetrated, our pelvic bones bumped repeatedly, his hand was on my ass, his mouth on my nipple, "It's so good mami." he's said over and over.

He felt so good inside of me, I felt pussy pulsating. He hit my g-spot and I tried not to scream, I moaned and bit his shoulder.

He lowered my leg. I was pressed against the wall. His hand in my hair with a nice grip as he kissed my mouth and then let his tongue lick my neck and found my breasts, "I'm about to cum." I said.

"I know," he replied and he dug deeper until I held him tightly.

"I wanna finish in the bed," he said.

I laughed, "Are you sure?"

He turned off the water stepped out of the shower and dried quickly. I stepped out and barely had a chance to dry off before went down and started licking me. I put my hand on the top of his head, "wait."

He stood up and held out his penis, I went down and tasted him while playing with his balls. His hands were on my head while he thrust inside of my mouth, seeing if I could accommodate all of him. "Let's go to the bed," he said.

I laid down and he got on top of me, looked down into my eyes, and started kissing me. I tried to wrap my legs around him, but he said, "No no, like this mami. I want you like this."

My legs straight, him between them, grinding deeper and deeper with every stroke. My heart raced, my forehead had beads of sweat, I had already wet the sheets and I felt like I was about to wet them some even more. He saw the look on my face and smiled, "Yeah mami."

I grabbed his ass and moaned, "Fuck Javi." I held him still inside of me and felt him releasing. We held that position for several seconds, just moaning and panting, still throbbing, I kissed his neck. I was so tired and worn out, I chuckled, "Oh my god."

He rolled off of me. I turned and looked at him, "I will have to leave in a few hours."

He looked at me, "You don't have to."

My purpose in stating that was, I was no longer interested in continuing to hide our relationship from Marco. I started to fall in love with the kid and since his ex was aware of me, I wanted to see how we could move forward.

"I do because Marco still thinks I'm just your *friend*." I got out of the bed and went into his bathroom to clean up. He entered the bathroom, "So, are you saying you want to tell my son that we're like a couple or something?"

I stared at him through the mirror, "I don't know exactly what this is. We started casually having sex and then you asked me to hang out with you and your son, so, I assumed—"

He shrugged, "I don't know."

"What don't you know?" I asked calmly.

"I like you. You know that."

I sighed, my eyebrows lifted and I shook my head, "I'm just trying to gauge how much effort I need to be putting into this. If you don't have any feelings for me like, you know, a girlfriend or whatever, that's fine. I just would like to know." I turned to look at him.

"I don't know Angie. You know I have a lot on my plate right now. Trying to raise my son alone, work, and keep his mom happy because she's mental."

I nodded and went into his room to find my clothes. He followed me, "So you're leaving? I guess I won't hear from you for another two or three months."

"You won't have to hear from me ever again," I replied as I put my shirt on.

He walked up to me, "Angie don't be like this. Don't run away."

I hated when people offered you terrible options and expected you to be like, "Yay, this is awesome." Like no sir, I'm not running from anything. I'm choosing myself over bullshit. I hugged him, "I'm not running away. I'm walking away from a situation before it becomes too painful." I stepped back and smiled, "take care of yourself."

And I left.

# Chapter 16: WTF (Jay)

On April 16<sup>th</sup>, I was in my shop, chilling in my office. Trish called, "Hey babe, I still need the names for the guest list."

I coughed and responded, "I'm working on that right now, I'll send it in an hour." The call ended.

Truth was, I wasn't working on the list. I wasn't excited about the whole situation. And it wasn't because Trish wasn't a good woman. It just felt like I don't know. I was still in my head about what happened with Angie and wondered why she just dropped off, changed her number.

I had been working on a project. I remembered her saying her birthday was in April. I smiled as I opened the book and flipped through the pages. I was certain, if I dug hard enough, I could find her parents' place in Tampa or, maybe just go see Cheyenne. I hadn't talked to her in a while either. Maybe she knew something.

I was scheduled to get married in June, right after Trish's son got out of school. And I bet you're wondering how it came to be that Trish and I were engaged. Let me tell you, after Christmas, Trish pretty much stayed posted up at my place.

She had transferred her job from Lakeland to Orlando and let her son go live with the father until the end of the school year. We were going at it pretty hard. I mean, she was there, in my bed every night. Now, before, when we first started, she was on the pill and I used condoms anyway, but one night, I was drunk off my ass and we ended up going at it...even though I was ready to start seeing another woman I had met in February, Trish told me that she was pregnant.

I was like, "wow." I didn't know how to feel. I wanted to be a father, but with someone, I wanted to be with for a long time. Someone that I vibed with and that person wasn't Trish.

She was nice, but she was serious most of the time. And whenever I joked with her, she sometimes got in her feelings. It was like constantly trying to not say the wrong thing.

My mother said she was a good woman and that no relationship was perfect that you have to learn people and get used to them. So, there it was, Trish was pregnant with my child and I hadn't heard from Angie...it just made some kind of sense.

As I was sitting there trying to write down some names, I got a notification from the gram that said, Cheyenne had posted. I opened up, looked at her page, and saw that she posted a picture of her and Angie.

And Angie looked good, vibrant, her hair was longer and her body was insane. This made me want to go holla at Cheyenne to see what was up. I had a few clients coming in, but I called them and rescheduled before heading to Cheyenne's place.

I walked into the coffee shop; I saw it was close to closing time. Cheyenne saw me and smiled, "Jay, I haven't seen you in a minute." She hugged me, "what are you doing here?" she asked, but before I could respond she congratulated me, "I heard about you and Trish and the baby."

I just looked at her. She squinted, "What's up?" She asked.

"Why you didn't tell me that you had heard from Angie?" I asked somewhat hurt.

She shrugged and her eyes widened, "I didn't think you...I mean, Angie said that she tried to see you back in December and that Trish said you and her were together."

I made a confused face, "what? When did Angie talk to Trish?"

"On Christmas Eve. She came through on her way to Tampa. Stopped at your spot and was told, you were no longer available. So, I just figured—"

"Ahhhhh," I said annoyed and pissed. I remembered that night. My mom had told me a woman visited and Trish had said it was a delivery person. Cheyenne stared at me as I anguished in my thoughts.

"Jay, do you still have a thing for Angie?" She asked.

My heart was so heavy. I had had a thing for Angie the first time I saw her. And here I was about to marry another woman that was carrying my child. How was I going to get Angie and how was I going to let down Trish? "Where is Angie?"

"Jay." She sighed, "Angie asked about you." She said.

I almost cried, "You told her?"

"Well, yeah."

"Fuck, fuck fuck." That was all I could say. If only I had taken that night off if only, I had made Trish go back to her place, so many ifs…

"She went to Tampa to pack up the rest of her stuff. She said she might be moving to LA."

"Can I get the address?"

"In Tampa?"

"Yes."

"What are you going to do Jay? You're getting married in a couple of months and have a baby on the way." She shook her head, "Angie is not going to stand in the way of you getting married."

"I can't marry Trish. I'm in love with Angie. So, just give me her address."

She took her phone and texted it to me. Before I left, I said, "Please don't tell her that I'm on my way. I need to talk to her."

She nodded. I hugged her and left.

# Chapter 17: The Best Surprise (Angela)

Usually, when I felt hella sad, I'd drown myself in Cold Stone Creamery, but, it was late and they were already closed. I went to my mom and dad's place. I didn't want to divulge all the details of my love life to her. As far as she knew, I was just upset about what happened with Corey.

I lay next to her in her huge king-sized bed, she played in my hair, speaking to me in Spanish. I just cried. I did feel bad about Corey. Mainly because I didn't see him as an abusive type.

I felt bad about what had transpired between Javier and me. The realization that he was just playing games and refused to set boundaries with his baby's mother. And most importantly, I bawled my eyes out because I had missed my chance with Jay and I had never stopped loving him.

Maybe the situation with Javier didn't pan out because I had never really addressed my feelings for Jay before moving on to someone new. But it was already too late to even try. What could I do if he was getting married and having a child?

Even though my parents insisted I was in no condition to head to my apartment in Ybor and they certainly weren't on board with me moving to LA. And honestly, I didn't want to be that far away from them. I had missed my life, my sisters, my old job. I got out of my mother's bed and said, "I just need to clear my head." I kissed them and left.

When I got to my apartment, I saw in front of my door, a gift bag with balloons. My first thoughts were *Corey* and I almost kicked it to the moon, but something urged me to take it inside, so I did.

I went inside to the counter in my kitchen, looked into the bag, pull out this book from the tissue that covered it. I opened it and immediately, my eyes watered and my heart was full. Page one, a drawing of the skyline of New Orleans.

Page two, me at the counter checking in that first night. I was wearing a sweater dress with boots and an infinity scarf. I had no idea he had ever seen me that night. Page three, us on the elevator, page four, us walking down Canal Street, and just pages of memories we had shared. I pulled out my cellphone, I sent him a text message, "Hey."

I saw the dots appear, "Hey." He texted back and then I heard a knock on my door. I thought, *is he here?* I hurried to the door and there he stood. I threw my arms around him and melted into him, "Thank you." I repeated. I held him in my arms, enjoyed the scent of him. It's something about being in the arms of a man that loves you exactly how you desire to be loved.

I stepped back and smiled, "Come in, do you need to use the bathroom, are you thirsty?"

He smiled, "Nah, I'm good."

We walked into the kitchen. I picked up the book, "Thank you for this. I didn't even know you saw me that first night."

"Hard not to notice the most beautiful woman in the lobby." He replied, his eyes had this sorrow, "I didn't know that you stopped by on Christmas Eve. I wish you would have called me."

My eyes watered, "I wanted to, but I figured what was the point. She was there and your parents were there. I figured I had missed my chance."

He stepped closer to me, "I'm here." I nodded as I looked into his soulful brown eyes, "but what does that mean? How do you see me fitting into everything you have going on? I don't want to share you."

"You don't have to." He replied and then kissed me. His lips felt so familiar and amazing.

I looked into his eyes, "but what about Trish and the baby?" I asked....

# Chapter 18: A Path Forward (Jay)

Almost one year later, my baby sat in my shop across from me while I tattooed roses and butterflies on her forearm. When I looked up to see if she was doing alright, her eyes made me feel warm inside. It's something about the way a woman looks at you, like, she feels completely comfortable and secure with you. And she was giving me that look and then she smiled with the dimples, which made me smile, "You aight ma?" I asked.

She nodded, "I'm good." I was just about finished. She asked me to tattoo her for her birthday and of course, I had to hook my baby up. Now, I bet you wondering how we got to this point.

That night, before I went to Tampa to see Angie, I went home to see Trish. Now, I wasn't mad, mad, but I was mad. She wasn't expecting me to get home early. Usually, on Fridays, I worked late.

I went in from the front door, I heard her voice and another woman's voice, they were sitting in the den. I heard her friend say, "So what are you going to do when he starts asking why you're not showing?"

At that moment, I knew something was off about the whole thing. That night she said we slept together without protection; I couldn't even remember it. And I ain't never been that drunk to where I couldn't remember being all up inside a woman. After that day, she kept trying to get me to have sex without protection and whenever I asked her about the doctor's appointments, she'd always make up some excuse about why she had to do it at certain times.

When I would rearrange my schedule to go with her, she'd say the appointment was canceled. I never would have thought Trish to be that kind of person. She was a nice little country southern girl, raised in the church. But then again, she did lie about Angela not visiting me on Christmas eve.

I listened closely as she told her friend, "I'll just say that I lost the baby, and then eventually after we get married, I can get pregnant. I just have to get him to the alter. He's a good man. I mean. He'll take care of me."

"I hear you girl." Her friend replied. I made some noise while I was in the kitchen so she could realize I was there. She came out with her friend, both of them looked at me like they had a secret.

I grinned inside. She kissed my cheek, "Hey Kendrick, you're home."

I nodded, "yeah. I have to make a run to Tampa."

Her face scrunched up, "Tonight, why, what's in Tampa?"

"The person who came to visit me on Christmas Eve, you remember, the delivery person that looked a lot like the woman you were admiring on your phone." I watched her expression.

Her friend sighed, "I have to get going." She left with the quickness.

When I heard the door close, I looked at her, "so what's up?"

"You didn't tell me you knew her and that you were seeing her." She said with her hand on her hip.

I shrugged, "Was I supposed to? Weren't you supposed to be getting back with your baby's father...or at least that's what you told me before my trip to New Orleans?"

She huffed, "Why her?"

"Because of her."

"So just like that? What about—"

"I know you're not pregnant. I heard you talking to your friend. That's fucked up."

She started crying, "You hardly even gave us a chance. If I would have told you that she came, you just would have run off to be with her."

"Damn right. I'm in love with that woman."

"How? I don't understand. We were together long before you met her."

I shrugged, "What do you even like about me, besides the fact that I can provide for you financially."

It was like her mind drew a blank. And don't get me wrong, I know as a man I'm supposed to take care of me and mine and I'm all about that, but this day and age when women are already doing for themselves, I wanted to know what else she saw in me.

We didn't laugh at the same jokes, she didn't like to travel or go out and always gave me flack about hanging out, even though I'd invite her and she damn sure didn't match my sexual energy. We were on two different pages.

"So that's it, I changed my whole life to come here to be with you and you're just going to go?"

I nodded. "I'll give you a few minutes to grab some stuff and we can work on a date for you to come by to get the rest." She ran up on me and tried to hit me. I was like seriously, girl you weigh 110 pounds. I picked her up and carried her out the door, "Get in your car, now." I said sternly.

She bawled, "I'm sorry. Please."

"I can call the police because right now, you're trespassing."

"Where am I supposed to go?"

I scoffed, "Are you serious. You make damn good money and I haven't asked you to pay not one bill since you posted up in my spot. Get a hotel, stay with a friend, figure it out."

She yelled, "I hate you!" Then she spat in my direction. It took everything in me not to snatch her lil ass up.

"Get in your car, Trish." I watched as she got in, she peeled out of my driveway wildly. I got in my car made sure she left and hurried to change the setting on the gate access code. She wasn't about to get back in and tear up my shit.

That night I drove out to Tampa to see Angie. I left the gift on her doorstep and waited in my car. Then when I received her text, I knew it was a good sign to go knock.

When she hugged me and I took one sniff of her hair, mango and shea butter, coconut oils, I felt at home. Then when I explained why she didn't have to share me with anyone, let's just say, we set that damn apartment on fire. Ooh wee if those walls could talk, triple X rated, mature audiences only.

She put her right hand in my locs, looked right in my eyes, brought my mouth to hers, and gave me the sexiest kiss, her tongue in my mouth, sucking my bottom lip, while she reached inside of my pants and massaged me until I was at attention. All I kept thinking was *fuck yeah, THIS!!!*

She had on one of those cute yellow sundresses, spaghetti straps, shorts, which showed off her legs, my hands slid under pulled off her panties, then I went down. It had been so long since I tasted her and she was just as sweet as I remembered. I ice-skated with the tip of my tongue on her clit until she flinched, buckled, and called my name. I stood, looked into her eyes, "You act like you forgot how I do."

She smiled, "I didn't forget. Let's go to the room."

We stood in front of each other, our bodies bare, she wrapped her arms around me and just held me, "I love you," she said.

I kissed the top of her head, "I love you too ma." I got in bed. She got in and was about to taste me, but I wanted some more of her, "Bring that ass up here while you do that," I said.

There she was, reminding me how she got down and could make my toes curl, while I was tasting her, and gripping all that juicy ass.

When I finished, I tapped her left cheek and she moved down and rode me backward. I loved watching her from behind, seeing her back, her ass wobble as she moved up and down on me. I reached around and touched her just before pulling her back so she could lay, her back to my chest. I held her hips in place, while I grinded underneath, "I missed you, Angie."

"I missed you too baby." She replied in her sweet alto. I turned her to her side, lifted her leg, and stroked her until I felt her leg shake, then I got on top, looked down into her eyes, and kissed while I penetrated and dug deep inside and paused. I heard her say, "ooooohhhhhh." I chuckled, she smiled, "You know what you be doing," she joked.

I laughed, "Yeah." I kept pushing and then I felt her legs wrap around me, "Baby, oh, shit." She came again and then I erupted inside of her. I forgot even to ask if she was still on the pill, but I was completely okay if she were to get pregnant.

I looked down into her eyes she smiled, "I'm still on the pill."

I laughed, "Nah, I wasn't worried about that. I love you."

Her hand reached up and touched the side of my face, she pulled me in and kissed me, "I love you too."

And the next day, she drove with me to Orlando and we had been kicking it since. Now, I won't act like everything was perfect, it took some getting used to, her being excessively neat, I had to give up some closet space, and then finally, I ended up moving most of my clothes to another room and made it my closet. But we had fun together.

We would have movie nights, and I'd lay with my head in her lap while she massaged my scalp. We would go to Cheyenne's club for open mic night, we'd travel, we even went to New York so she could meet my parents and my mom ended up loving her because Angie could eat and wasn't shy. And my mom loved to cook.

Now, it took her mom a little while to warm up to me. You know, I'm a completely different look from the last guy she met, that dated Angie. But I'll never forget the day we were at her parents' house in Tampa and her mom said to her, "You look happy m'ija."

Angie hugged her mom, "I am." And from that moment, she started softening up. Her dad was cool from the start. We would sit and talk sports for hours while drinking beer.

This year, for Angie's birthday, I planned a trip to New Orleans. I want to ask her the most important question of our lives in the place where it all started.

# About the Author

Marianna Love is a Florida-based writer who channels her alter-ego to create content that stimulates her readers. She enjoys bringing diversity into her writing with a heavy influence on interracial and multi-ethnic relationships.

Read more at https://eroticawithmariannalove.wordpress.com.